THEY WOULD ~~LEAVE A BLOOD-RED~~
TRAIL OF H~~OT LEAD AND COLD~~
D~~EATH...~~

CAPTAIN VINCENT BOLTON—the famed Indian fighter and gallant soldier who is ordered into dangerous territory on a mission of blood and love. What he discovers is the tortured town of Socorro—the town where evil lives and goes by the name of Big Jim Congor.

SEÑORITA ARABELLA CHRISTINA ALBARA Y CARRANZA—the proud and lovely daughter of a Spanish nobleman who is on a sacred mission to find his ancestor's remains in the gold-laden Gran Quivira Mission. But her personal mission could end in surprising love . . . or violent death.

ANTONIO MONTERO—his daughter was stolen from his home by Big Jim Congor to be used in Congor's notorious bordello. When Antonio asks Big Jim to return his daughter, he makes the final mistake of his life.

BIG JIM CONGOR—the vicious, big-money guntough and killer who holds the town of Socorro in a grip of fear. Only one man has ever dared to come up against him: Captain Vincent Bolton. Now Congor will not rest until Bolton and all his traveling companions are six feet under their mission of gold.

The Stagecoach Series
Ask your bookseller for the books you have missed

STAGECOACH STATION 44:
SOCORRO

Hank Mitchum

Created by the producers of
**Wagons West, Stagecoach,
Abilene, and Faraday.**

Book Creations Inc., Canaan, NY · Lyle Kenyon Engel, Founder

BANTAM BOOKS
NEW YORK · TORONTO · LONDON · SYDNEY · AUCKLAND

SOCORRO
A BANTAM BOOK / PUBLISHED BY ARRANGEMENT WITH
BOOK CREATIONS, INC.

PRODUCED BY BOOK CREATIONS, INC.
LYLE KENYON ENGEL, FOUNDER

BANTAM EDITION / NOVEMBER 1989
ALL RIGHTS RESERVED.
COPYRIGHT © 1989 BY BOOK CREATIONS, INC.
COVER ART COPYRIGHT © 1989 BY GUY DEEL.

ISBN 0-553-28257-3

Published simultaneously in the United States and Canada

Bantam Books are published by Bantam Books, a division of Bantam
Doubleday Dell Publishing Group, Inc. Its trademark, consisting of the
words "Bantam Books" and the portrayal of a rooster, is Registered in U.S.
Patent and Trademark Office and in other countries. Marca Registrada,
Bantam Books, 666 Fifth Avenue, New York, New York 10103

PRINTED IN THE UNITED STATES OF AMERICA

O   0 9 8 7 6 5 4 3 2 1

STAGECOACH STATION 44:
SOCORRO

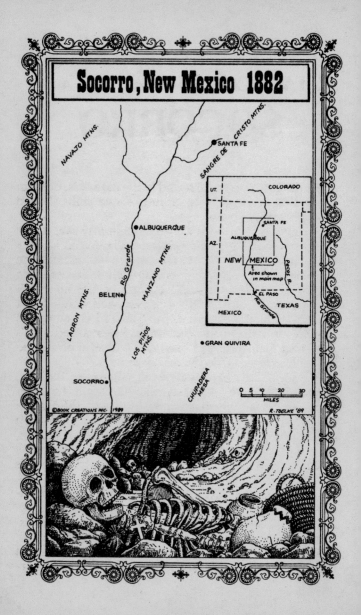

Chapter One

At the first whisper of sound in the darkness, Captain Vince Bolton stepped aside, just as two clubs slashed through empty space.

In the dim light from a livery stable fifty feet away, Vince could see his two attackers silhouetted as they charged from the alley. Grabbing the nearest one, he pulled him off balance and seized his club. The bearded man was compact and muscular, but he was no match for the captain, who stood over six feet and weighed just under two hundred pounds. As Vince's hat fell to the ground, he twisted the club from the bearded man's hand and then thumped him on the head with it. The bearded man collapsed with a groan.

The second attacker, somewhat taller than the first, loomed in front of Vince, snarling an oath as he again swung his club. Vince parried the blow with the club he held and then slid it down the length of his opponent's club. As it raked the man's knuckles, he gasped in pain, dropping his weapon. Taking advantage of the man's momentary vulnerability, Vince rammed the end of his club into his stomach, knocking the breath from him. The man clutched his belly as he doubled over, sprawling beside his companion.

The scuffle had been quick and quiet, scarcely disturbing the stillness of the narrow side street in Socorro, New Mexico Territory. Years of leading cavalry patrols in hostile territory had made the tall, thirty-two-year-

1

old army man constantly aware of his surroundings, always ready to react to a threat. Tossing the club aside, Vince picked up his campaign hat, dusted it off, and placed it back on his auburn head. He reached into his pants pocket and pulled out a match, which he struck against the sole of his boot. When the light flared, he could see that the two men were ragged and scruffy, similar to other newcomers he had seen wandering about Socorro's streets since he had arrived home on leave from his regiment the day before.

It had not taken Vince long to see that the town had changed during his absence. His father, the manager of the Socorro way station for the Rio Grande Stagecoach Company, had told him that a man called Big Jim Congor had taken up residence and established a saloon, making it the headquarters for his gang of riffraff. Through extortion, Congor had gained ownership of Socorro's only hotel, which he had turned into a bordello. There he kept many women who had been forced into his sordid employ because of loans Congor had given them or their families at usurious rates.

Vince suspected that Big Jim Congor was behind the attack that had just taken place. The previous day, shortly after arriving in Socorro, he had argued with Congor over an incident that had taken place outside of Congor's hotel. Vince had seen the big man slapping a young woman, who was crying for him to let her go. When the captain had intervened on the woman's behalf, Congor had told him to mind his own business, claiming that the woman had deserved what he had given her. When Vince had asked the woman if what Congor said was true, she had glanced fearfully at Congor and then, with downcast eyes, claimed that he had not done anything to her against her will. Unable to help the woman without cooperation, Vince had walked away, but not before he warned Congor that he had not seen the last of Vince Bolton.

When Vince had informed his father about the incident, Harvey Bolton had told him to keep his eyes peeled for trouble; Big Jim Congor was not the kind of man to let a dispute end with words.

Vince thought of his father's warning as he examined his attackers, who were still lying on the ground. The bearded man was dazed, and blood was streaming from a gash on his forehead. The other was wheezing and gripping his stomach, trying to catch his breath. Vince nudged him with his boot. "How much did Congor pay you?" he asked.

The reply was an oath that changed into a howl of pain as the heel of Vince's cavalry boot dug into his ribs. "I don't know what you're talking about," the man growled, shrinking away.

"Yes, you do. How much did Congor pay you to track me down?"

"You've got it wrong, mister," the man protested. "Me and my friend here wanted to get some money, but we picked the wrong mark."

Knowing the man was lying for fear of retaliation from Congor, Vince told him to stand up and get his friend on his feet. Rising, the man asked warily, "Are you going to take us to jail?"

"No," Vince grunted as he nudged the other man with his boot. "I see no reason for the taxpayers to feed you. I'm going to have a talk with Congor, and you're coming with me."

"No, I ain't!" the man exclaimed, turning to flee. "You ain't going to get me into trouble with Big Jim!"

Catching the man's arm, Vince spun him around and slammed a right into his belly. The man reeled back against the building at the corner of the alley, and Vince punched him in the face. Sagging on his feet, with blood gushing from his mouth and nose, the man offered no further resistance. He helped his companion to his feet, and then the two of them staggered along the street as Vince prodded them from behind.

At this time of night it was quiet in the central part of the town, where narrow streets passed between adobe buildings that had been built around a seventeenth-century Spanish mission. Now, in 1882, a lively farming and livestock center, Socorro was inhabited mostly by lawful, hardworking people who rose early and were in bed soon after nightfall. There was more activity on the newer west side of the town, where a number of businesses in recently·constructed wooden buildings catered to prospectors and laborers from the nearby silver mines. Vince steered the two men in that direction.

Passersby looked with curiosity at the tall, muscular captain in his trim cavalry uniform as he herded the two battered men down the street toward the Sundowner Saloon. Blazing with light, it was a bedlam of raucous laughter, bellowing voices, and loud music. As he pushed the men through the batwing doors and stepped in behind them, Vince realized that word of the plan to attack him must have reached the saloon before him, judging from the reaction of its patrons. Those lining the bar turned to look, and seeing that Vince had come out of the brawl in better shape than the attackers, they fell quiet.

Congor was on the far side of the saloon, at a table with some of his gang. Although he was about the same height as Vince, years of indolence and unbridled appetite had turned his muscles into flab. He wore a flashy suit of bright checkered wool that was buttoned tautly over his bulging stomach.

Vince pushed the two men toward Congor and stood behind them. Stiff with fright, they cowered as they faced the big man's furious glare. When Vince gave them a final shove toward Congor's table, both of them stumbled and fell heavily to the floor.

"These two can't even stay on their feet, Congor," Vince remarked contemptuously. "Are they the best you could find to do your dirty work?"

His beady eyes glaring malignantly, a sardonic smile spread over Congor's doughy face as he shook his head. "What are you talking about, Bolton?" he sneered in a raspy voice. "I've never seen those two men before."

"You're a liar, Congor," Vince retorted. "You're a liar as well as a coward, too yellow to face anyone yourself."

Congor's fat face slowly turned crimson, his sagging chins quivering with fury. A stir passed through the men scattered about the saloon, and those at the table looked to Congor as if for guidance on what to do about the point-blank insult.

Vince, smiling humorlessly, glanced around the bar. "No, you can relax, you worthless scum," he said. "You should know by now that Congor wouldn't want you to do anything here. He's too cowardly to do anything in the open." Turning back to Congor, Vince pointed a finger in warning. "If it happens again, Congor, I won't end it by dealing with your hired thugs. I'll deal directly with you." He stared at Congor stonily for a moment and then turned and left, his footsteps and the jingle of his cavalry spurs loud in the stillness. As he pushed through the batwing doors, the quiet behind him was shattered by an explosion of indignant bellows and oaths.

Shrugging off his anger, Vince walked away from the west end of Socorro and back through the quiet, dark streets to the stagecoach way station. Adjacent to the old road that stretched from El Paso to Santa Fe, the station was a compound of barns, quarters for overnight passengers, and other buildings, all enclosed within an adobe wall. As he walked through the wide front gate, Vince saw that his father was sitting on the porch of the office, talking with Alfred Buell, Socorro's marshal and a friend of the Bolton family for many years.

The resemblance between father and son was quite striking. Vince had inherited his father's blue eyes and auburn hair, as well as his rugged features. A widower in his fifties, Harvey Bolton was a lean, gray-bearded man, as tall as his son. He had once owned a large ranch in the southern part of the territory but had sold it years ago after being severely injured in a stampede. The injury had left him with a limp, but he was financially comfortable and had taken the job as way station manager primarily to keep busy.

Marshal Buell, a grizzled, leathery man of middle age, greeted Vince and added that he was relieved to see him. "I know you can take care of yourself, Vince, but you'd better keep an eye on your back. When I was at the Sundowner a couple of hours ago, I heard some miners say they had heard that Congor might be sending men after you."

Taking a seat, Vince replied that Congor had done just that, and then he described what had happened. As he talked, he was acutely aware that his father often sat on the porch on balmy summer evenings like this one. A lantern illuminated the porch, while the inky darkness at the adobe wall enclosing the way station would provide the perfect cover for a gunman.

"My main worry, Dad, is that you may become involved in my trouble with Congor. He's cowardly enough to use you as a way to get even with me, and you'd make a good target while sitting on this porch."

Laughing dryly, Harvey Bolton replied, "He's cowardly enough, but not crazy enough. If anyone took a shot at me, the Rio Grande Stagecoach Company would have territorial lawmen here the next day. Congor knows that, and it's about the last thing he would want."

The marshal nodded in agreement. "You're right. Big Jim Congor doesn't want to draw any attention to himself. He lends out money here and there in order to gain control over people, and he's behind some other dirty schemes as well. But my hands are tied, because I can't get anybody who's had trouble with him even to talk about it. Everybody is afraid to come forward and be a witness against him."

"Then the trouble he has with me is a real problem for him," Vince mused. "He controls people through fear. I've stood up to him, and if he doesn't take some sort of measure against me, others might be encouraged to come forward as witnesses."

The marshal pursed his lips, nodding thoughtfully.

"Yes, I hadn't looked at it in exactly that way, but you're right, Vince. This could turn out to be what I've hoped for, a chance to rid Socorro of Congor. But he knows it, too, so you'd better be mighty careful."

"Congor has a lot more to worry about than Vince does," Harvey Bolton remarked confidently. "For the past couple of years, Vince has been up against Geronimo and the Chiricahuas in Arizona Territory, so he can look after himself. But Congor and his bunch of varmints are sneaky and sly, so you do need to watch your back, Vince."

Buell nodded in agreement and then, eyeing Vince slyly, introduced another subject. "I thought that by now you'd be bringing a wife and children with you when you come home to visit, Vince. You're a handsome young fellow, so I know there must be plenty of young ladies who'd welcome your attentions."

"Not in Arizona Territory," Vince replied, laughing. "Anyway, I'm a soldier first and last, Marshal Buell. That doesn't leave me with the time or opportunity for other things, including marriage."

"Vince is married to the army, Fred," Harvey put in, "and he has been ever since he went to West Point. As you say, he's fine looking, but he might as well be as ugly as a gila monster for all the help his looks are in getting a wife."

The marshal laughed and then got up and said good night.

Harvey continued to chide Vince about his being single at the age of thirty-two. "I'll probably go to my grave without ever seeing a grandchild," he said with a chuckle as he bid his son good night.

Vince's mother had died when he was in his early teens, and he had thrown all his energies into his duties on his father's ranch. By the age of fifteen he was working day and night, helping Harvey to the point where he at times took on the parental role. He had grown up too fast, never allowing himself time to develop friendships, let alone a romance—perhaps to protect himself from suffering the same loss his father had. That same sense of duty had carried over to the fight against Geronimo, and now to Congor. But it did not occur to Vince as he lay in bed that night that there was more to life than fulfilling his responsibilities to his father and his country.

That night Vince slept as he did on patrol, ready to be alert immediately upon hearing any unusual sound.

If Big Jim Congor intended to do anything, he was biding his time, for the night passed without incident. Early the next morning Vince had breakfast with his father in the way station dining room and then went to help the handyman change the teams on the stage that was due in shortly.

A gangling man in his thirties, Jake Clinton was taking the horses from their stalls in the stables. While not overly intelligent, Clinton was carefree and irrepressibly cheerful, and he grinned at Vince as he stepped into the stables. "Good morning, Vince," he called genially. "Did you sleep good?"

"Yes, I did, Jake," Vince answered. "Did you?"

"You bet I did," the man replied happily. "I never slept bad in my life."

"I expect you're far better off than most people, Jake. Which horses are you taking out?"

The man pointed to the horses. Vince took one of them out of the stall, and then he and Clinton led the animals from the stables. Presently, as they stood at one side of the front courtyard, the rumble of wheels and pounding of hoofbeats sounded.

The stage charged through the gate, and the driver leaned back on the reins, pulling the horses to a skidding stop. After the doors opened, the passengers climbed out stiffly as the driver bounded down from the box, touching his dusty hat to Vince in greeting. As the driver and passengers filed toward the way station dining room for breakfast, Vince and Clinton began to change the horses.

Once the sweaty, weary horses from the stage were in the corral beside the stables, Vince helped Jake pitch some fence posts until lunchtime, when he had time to ponder the situation with Congor. The man was a blight on what had been a peaceful, pleasant town, and Vince was eager to do anything he could to stop the man from ruining the lives of more citizens.

After lunch with his father, Vince went to his room to change into his uniform. He then saddled a horse and rode into Socorro, where he planned on spending the entire afternoon. He wanted to give Big Jim Congor ample opportunity to provoke him. If that happened, Vince intended to do whatever he could to put Congor behind bars.

After stopping several times on the streets to talk with acquaintances, Vince headed for the west side of town. As he passed a hardware store, a man whom Vince had known as a child was coming out.

The man was Juan Montero, owner of a small farm. Dark haired and short, Juan greeted Vince happily, shaking hands with him. "Vincent! It has been years since I saw you."

"It has been a while. How have you been, Juan?"

"I am fine, but the hot sun has made me thirsty. Will you let me buy you a drink, Vincent? The cantina is nearby."

Palming the sweat from his forehead, Vince agreed, and within a minute the two men were stepping into the darkness of the cantina. The thick adobe walls made the air inside cool on this warm afternoon, and the place was quiet, with only a couple of customers at the bar. Vince and Juan ordered glasses of beer and carried them to a table in a corner of the nearly deserted room. Sipping their beers, they exchanged news of events since they had last seen each other.

"How is your family, Juan? Last time I saw you, you had just bought out your brother's share of the farm. You must be pleased to have the entire spread for your family now." Vince knew that Juan and his brother,

Antonio, did not get along well. Antonio was an inveterate gambler and as lazy as Juan was energetic. When the two of them had inherited their father's farm, Juan had labored for years to pay what Antonio demanded for his share.

Juan became moody at the mention of his brother's name. "Antonio is no family of mine, the way I see it."

When Juan scowled and took a long swig of his beer, Vince decided to steer the subject back onto more positive ground. "Well, how is the farm doing, then?"

Juan was silent for a moment, and then he frowned somberly. "I will tell you something, Vincent, but you must not mention it to anyone else. Not a word."

"Whatever you say, Juan."

"Antonio finally found someone who would lend him plenty of money to gamble. That man is Big Jim Congor, and he owns Antonio now, body and soul. Do you remember Antonio's daughter?"

"Little Rosa?"

"Yes, Vincent. Well, little Rosa is now in Congor's whorehouse."

The sound of Congor's name made Vince's blood boil —and he was hearing that name all too often. He shook his head in disgust. "It's not right, Juan. She's only a girl."

"She is seventeen now," Juan said. He took another long swallow of beer. "When I heard about it, I went to Antonio, and he threatened my family if I told anyone. He is afraid that Congor will kill him if anyone makes trouble." Burying his forehead in his hands, he said in a voice filled with torment, "Vincent, my niece is in a whorehouse . . . and I can do nothing about it!"

"Well, I can. I'll get her out of there, Juan."

Juan looked up at Vince with hope. "How will you do that?"

Vince snarled with contempt for the man who was making so many lives miserable. "I'll walk in, take her by the arm, and drag her out. No one needs to know that you and I talked about this."

Sighing, Juan shook his head. "No, Vincent, you must not do that. Everyone would know. You are the only one who has challenged Congor, and everyone knows that you and I are friends. No. Antonio is afraid that Congor will kill him, and perhaps Congor would. I don't want my brother's blood on my hands."

As they finished their beers, Vince tried to think of a more indirect way to get the young woman out of the bordello immediately, but he could think of nothing. He did assure Juan, however, that he would bring his case to the marshal, and although Juan was appreciative, Vince could see that his friend was not optimistic.

After Juan and he had parted, the captain continued going from place to place in the town, giving Congor plenty of chances to make his move. Vince was more determined than ever to deal with the man, but when the afternoon had passed and there had been no sign of Congor or his men, he finally went back to the way station.

Harvey and the marshal were sitting on the porch when Vince arrived at sunset. He told them that he had not run into Congor and then described his talk with Juan Montero. "I offered to go after the girl in the bordello right away, but Juan was against it. He insisted that anyone who went after Rosa would be placing Antonio in grave danger."

The marshal thought for a moment and then said, "Vince, you shouldn't put yourself in any more danger where Congor is concerned. I'll look up Antonio soon and see what he has to say. I'll need a statement from him that his daughter is in there against her will, and if I get that, I'll confront Congor."

The men went inside for some dinner and ended up talking late into the night. When the marshal left, he again warned Vince to be careful about Congor.

The next morning Vince was again helping Jake Clinton with the horses when the southbound stage stormed into the compound with a cloud of dust and a roar of hoofbeats. As the driver climbed down from the box, he took an envelope from his pocket and called out, "Captain Bolton! I have a message for you. The adjutant at the garrison in Santa Fe asked me to deliver it to you."

Thanking the man, Vince took the envelope and opened it. It contained a letter from Colonel John Hamilton, the commander of army forces stationed in New Mexico Territory. The letter was brief, requesting that Vince come to Santa Fe and talk with the colonel on a matter of the utmost urgency.

Vince read the letter again, thinking the request was an unusual one. Normally any request the colonel made of him would be sent through channels to his regiment. If it was approved, his regimental commander would send him a message ending his leave and ordering him to report to Colonel Hamilton.

Vince was unhappy about ending his leave so abruptly. The trip to Santa Fe would interfere with his plan to rid Socorro of Big Jim Congor. But he had no choice; he had to do as the colonel asked.

Putting the letter in his pocket, he helped Jake finish harnessing the fresh horses to the coach. When the other horses were in the corral, Vince looked around for his father. Finding him outside the office, he showed him the letter.

Harvey read it and frowned in disappointment. "I was looking forward to having you around a little longer, Vince," he said. "Why do you think Colonel Hamilton wants to talk with you?"

"I have no idea, Dad," Vince said, "but I'll find out before very long. I'm going to collect my shaving gear and change into a clean uniform. I want to get started for Santa Fe right away."

"I'll saddle a horse for you, son."

Vince nodded his thanks, turning toward his room as his father left for the stables. Glancing over the letter once again, he speculated about what the colonel might have in mind for him. He had an uneasy feeling that it might turn out to be something that he would much rather avoid.

Chapter Two

Santa Fe was exactly the way Vince remembered it from the first time he had seen it as a young boy. It had remained unchanged through the years because it was a place where American innovation had come to a standstill, meeting with the inertia of centuries. The town had become a thriving Spanish colonial capital only a decade after the Pilgrims landed at Plymouth Rock, and its long history gave it an atmosphere of calm serenity that was rare in the burgeoning West.

From the time of his first visit, Vince had always had a special fondness for Santa Fe. Set on a high rolling tableland against a backdrop of the lofty Sangre de Cristo Mountains, it was a peaceful, picturesque town, the sparkling clear air sweet with the smell of piñon trees.

Vince approached the garrison on the outskirts of the town, and tethered his horse in front of the headquarters building and went inside, where a sergeant immediately escorted him into the office of Colonel John Hamilton. A tall, graying man with the briskly cordial manner of a senior officer, the colonel put aside a sheaf of paper to return Vince's salute and shake hands with him.

Colonel Hamilton stopped the sergeant as he turned to leave. "Sergeant Hoskins, have the carriage brought to the front entrance. Also, have Captain Bolton's horse taken to the stables and his belongings taken to his quarters. A room has been prepared for him, hasn't it?"

14

"Yes, sir. Just as you ordered."

"Very well." Hamilton turned back to Vince as the sergeant left. "Your promptness is commendable, Captain Bolton. I didn't expect you to get here until tomorrow, but I'm very pleased you arrived today."

"Your message said the matter was urgent, sir," Vince replied and then indirectly broached the question of why he had been summoned. "If quarters have been prepared for me, I presume I'll be here for a time."

"For a few days, perhaps," the colonel said vaguely. "Captain, I've been informed that you are a native of New Mexico Territory. Are you familiar with every region of it?"

"Yes, sir. I was born on a ranch in the southern part of the territory and grew up in Socorro. I guess I've been in just about every part of the territory at one time or another."

"Good," Hamilton said emphatically, taking his hat from a rack. "Let's go to the front entrance to wait for the carriage. We'll be going to the territorial governor's office."

"The territorial governor?" Vince echoed as he followed the colonel out the door.

"Everything will be made clear to you in good time, Captain Bolton. I understand that you're posted with the regiment in Arizona Territory. Geronimo and his warriors are quite a problem, aren't they?"

"Yes, sir," Vince agreed, and told the colonel of the latest developments as they made their way toward the front entrance. Once the carriage arrived, they climbed in and continued to discuss the campaign against the Chiricahuas in Arizona Territory as they rode through town to the cobblestoned central plaza.

The driver brought the carriage to a halt in front of the Palace of the Governors, the oldest building on the North American continent. Constructed of adobe and oak beams that were as enduring as stone, it was a small, modest building for its title, but its vast age was apparent. While it had been carefully maintained, the stone steps were worn by the footsteps of generations, and its outside walls bore scars from conflicts of previous centuries.

Hamilton led Vince inside and along a corridor to an anteroom outside the governor's office. There, the governor's secretary asked Hamilton to wait, explaining that the governor was in conference with the attorney general.

"Inform the governor that I'm here with Captain Bolton of Socorro," the colonel ordered the man firmly. "He will want to see us immediately."

The secretary tapped on the office door and then quietly stepped inside, closing it behind him. A moment later, he emerged ahead of a man who carried a thick folder of papers. The man, whom Vince surmised must be the attorney general, nodded amiably to Hamilton and him and left. The governor was right behind him, and he looked at Vince with keen interest as he came out of the office.

A portly, nattily dressed man in his late forties, Governor Lionel Sheldon shook hands with Vince and greeted him warmly as Hamilton introduced them. "Our information was correct, sir," the colonel said. "Captain Bolton grew up in the territory and is thoroughly familiar with it."

"I'm very pleased to hear that," the governor replied. "I'm also very grateful that you're here so soon, Captain Bolton." He looked Vince up and down again, nodding with satisfaction, and then turned back to his office. "Well, come in, gentlemen, and let's have a talk."

After leading the two officers into his spacious, well-furnished office overlooking the plaza, the governor gestured for Vince to have a seat in a chair near the desk. The colonel took another chair as Governor Sheldon sat down at his desk and opened a folder. "Now, to get directly to the matter at hand, we have a distinguished visitor from Spain here in Santa Fe, Captain Bolton. He is a Castilian grandee named Don Raimundo Arnulfo y Carranza."

The governor went on to explain who the man was, although Vince knew the name well. Several years before, Spain had gone through a period of open warfare between several factions that had been trying to gain control of the country. That strife had ended when Alphonse XII assumed the throne and united the nation, a process in which Don Raimundo had been a key figure.

"He's a fine old gentleman," Sheldon went on. "Quite hearty, despite being well into his seventies. His daughter, Señorita Arabella Christina Albara y Carranza, is here with him, along with a foreign ministry official and servants. Naturally, the goodwill of an individual in his position is very important to the United States." The governor removed a paper from the folder and handed it across the desk. "On that subject, please take a look at this letter, Captain Bolton."

The letter, written by the secretary of state in Washington and addressed to Governor Sheldon, was cordial in tone but firm and completely to the point. It stated that President Arthur's personal wish was that Don Raimundo and those accompanying him be extended all possible courtesy, cooperation, and assistance.

"Is Don Raimundo here on an official visit of some sort, sir?" Vince asked, passing the letter back to the governor.

"No, he's not," Governor Sheldon replied. "The official from the Spanish foreign ministry is with him to see that he is safe at all times and to act as an interpreter, but Don Raimundo is here for a personal reason. It concerns a member of his family from many generations ago, a priest named Eusebio Armero y Carranza. This priest was in charge of the mission at Gran Quivira when it was abandoned during the Indian uprising in 1680. Are you familiar with that event and the location of Gran Quivira, Captain Bolton?"

"Yes, sir. The Pueblo revolt. It was a general uprising all over the territory. Gran Quivira is south of here and east of the mountains along the Rio Grande, near the salt lakes. I went there a couple of times when I was a boy."

The governor nodded and then continued. "When the uprising occurred, Padre Eusebio set out for Mexico City, but he was never heard from again. During the following generations, the Carranza family has considered the lack of knowledge about Padre Eusebio's fate to be a severe stigma on them. That's why Don Raimundo is here, and that's where you come in, Captain Bolton."

"Where I come in, sir?" Vince asked, just as puzzled as ever.

"Yes. You see, Don Raimundo wants to locate his relative's remains and have them interred in hallowed ground. We would like you to act as guide for him and his party, and to help him find the priest's remains."

The request was couched in polite terms, but nevertheless Vince felt the underlying pressure in the governor's words. Yet he was sure Governor Sheldon could not be fully aware of the dangers they would surely encounter on such a journey. Vince was silent, carefully considering his response.

"I see you have reservations," Sheldon remarked urbanely. "You can imagine our dilemma when Don Raimundo arrived and we were unable to find anyone we could entrust with this responsibility. Colonel Hamilton found out you were on leave in Socorro, and it turns out that your qualifications are excellent. If you will do this, it will be deeply appreciated by everyone here as well as by the senior officials in Washington. So let's discuss your reservations and see how they can be resolved."

"Very well, sir," Vince replied, though he was wondering where to start. "First, searching thousands of square miles of wasteland for the remains of someone who died there two hundred years ago would be an extremely difficult task, if not futile. That is some of the worst terrain in the Southwest, with midday temperatures that are savagely hot. Taking an aged man, his daughter, and their tenderfoot party on such a trip would be unwise, to say the least. Not to mention that for the past few years unfriendly Mescaleros have been roaming that region."

"But they haven't attacked anyone, Captain Bolton," Hamilton quickly pointed out. "The worst they've done is to steal livestock, and they always travel in small foraging parties that spread out from their base camp in Mexico."

Vince's experience with Geronimo had taught him never to underestimate the dangers of traveling in the wilderness. He felt that Hamilton's cavalier attitude was not very realistic.

Again Vince chose his words carefully. "I don't think it's wise to risk lives on the expectation that they will never attack anyone, sir. Also, their being in small bands is still a threat. I know their chief, White Eagle, and he's a cautious man. I wouldn't be concerned if the Mescaleros traveled as one group, since he would always be in control. But a leading warrior in command of a small party, away from White Eagle's influence, might have a score to settle or just decide to take a few scalps."

Governor Sheldon leaned back in his chair and clasped his hands behind his head. "Those are good points that you've brought up, Captain Bolton." A moment later he brought his arms forward, rested them on his desk, and continued, "Let's take them one at a time. In regard to the potential danger from Indians, Colonel Hamilton and I have already agreed that a cavalry escort will accompany the party."

"How large an escort, sir?"

"A full patrol, twenty troopers and a sergeant. Regarding the terrain and the weather, I discussed this with Don Raimundo through his interpreter, and he assured me it isn't a concern. I'm inclined to accept that. Don Raimundo is a tough old man, and Señorita Arabella appears more capable of enduring hardships than many men. In any event, we really aren't in a position to tell them what they can or can't endure, are we?"

Raising his eyebrows with resignation, Vince replied, "I suppose not, sir."

"Now, the remaining issue is the difficulty of searching such a large area. In letters he wrote to his family in Spain, Padre Eusebio described a private place where he occasionally withdrew to meditate. Don Raimundo feels certain his relative went there and met his end, so the search will be limited to that place. It's a mesa where ancient Indian ruins are located, just a day's journey from Gran Quivira."

"That raises another very serious problem, sir," Vince interrupted. "The place you just described is Chupadera Mesa, which is sacred to Indians. If we're spotted there, White Eagle and all his warriors will be after us in no time."

"I pride myself on respecting Indians' beliefs," the governor countered, "but in all sincerity, I don't think that looking about for a priest's remains would be desecrating a sacred place. You say you know White Eagle, Captain, so surely you could explain it to him if he happened to find you there, couldn't you?"

"I don't believe he would consider the explanation adequate, sir. I've known him since I was a boy, but our relationship is one of mutual respect, not friendship. If it came down to a conflict, White Eagle would lift my scalp just as quickly as anyone else's."

Colonel Hamilton shifted his position in his chair and said, "Well, if it comes down to a conflict, you'll have a cavalry troop, Captain Bolton. You're an experienced cavalry officer, so that's a situation I'm sure you can deal with."

"Yes, and any other situation," Governor Sheldon added confidently. "Is there anything else you would like to bring up, Captain?"

"Yes, sir," Vince stated abruptly. He was feeling a bit perturbed that his arguments were being dismissed so quickly. "By legend, Gran Quivira was the wealthiest mission in the territory. All of the gold altar vessels and other valuables disappeared during the Pueblo revolt and were never seen again. If outlaw gangs find out about Don Raimundo's destination, they'll conclude that he knows where the gold is and that he's after it, at least as a secondary purpose. In that event, an ambush by outlaws on the return trip is very likely. How widespread is the knowledge of Don Raimundo's plans?"

Considering the issue a serious one, the governor said, "Well, it couldn't be very widespread. The Carranzas and their party have kept very much to themselves, and Don Raimundo declined a newspaper interview. The only ones I've mentioned it to are my immediate staff."

"I've mentioned it only to my staff as well, sir," Hamilton volunteered.

"And we'll clap the lid on that information right now," the governor announced firmly. "Colonel Hamilton, let's advise our staffs to let it go no further, and from here on we'll treat it as confidential information. That will keep it from the wrong ears, Captain Bolton."

"Yes, sir," Vince said, although he did not feel as confident as he sounded.

"Captain, this has been a very enlightening meeting," the governor said in conclusion. "I told Don Raimundo that we intended to ask you to escort him, and he's been looking forward to meeting you. I've invited him to my home for dinner this evening, and I'd like you two gentlemen to be my guests as well. His interpreter will be there, so you can discuss the entire situation with him in detail, Captain Bolton."

"An interpreter won't be necessary, sir. I speak fluent Mexican Spanish, which is very similar to Castilian."

"Excellent," the governor said, rising. "Captain, I see that in you we've had the exceeding good fortune of finding just the right man for the job. I can't express how pleased I am. I'll expect you gentlemen at my home at about seven this evening, then."

After Vince had shaken hands with the governor, he followed Colonel Hamilton out of the office. He had many misgivings about the situation, and his objections had been brushed aside far too quickly to suit him.

Early evening had settled over Santa Fe as Vince Bolton and John Hamilton rode to the governor's house in the garrison carriage. In the stillness at the end of the day, the smell of woodsmoke from cooking fires blended with the scent of piñon trees, and the last rays of sunlight lingered on the peaks of the mountains. Vince scarcely noticed the spectacular setting, however. He was pondering the dangers that would face the Spaniards once they set out in search of their ancestor's remains.

"Dealing with hostile Indians isn't all that bad," he mused aloud to the colonel. With a wry smile he added, "I wish you had sent for me to track down White Eagle instead of leading this unusual search party, sir."

Hamilton laughed and then replied sympathetically, "In your position, I'd feel the same. Being nursemaid to a party of civilians isn't a job that any soldier would stand in line for, but your qualifications are even better than we had hoped. And you saw yourself what that letter from Washington said."

"Yes, sir. But the collective knowledge of the West in Washington wouldn't match that of the rawest recruit at the garrison, and the President certainly wouldn't want us to get those people killed. Considerations of human life aside, it would be an extreme discredit to the nation."

"That's quite true. However, as the governor told you, he's explained the dangers of the undertaking to Don Raimundo."

"Through an interpreter. I have to wonder if the governor's full meaning was conveyed to Don Raimundo, sir, because it just doesn't seem logical that a man would take his daughter into such circumstances."

The colonel pursed his lips thoughtfully and then slowly nodded. "Well, you'll have full opportunity to talk with him yourself tonight. Bear in mind, though, that he seems determined to do this, even at the risk of his life and his daughter's. That being the case, the only alternative to your escorting them is a civilian guide, who might be half drunk all of the time. You're the one man who can do the best job of protecting them."

Acknowledging that point, Vince fell silent. There had been an undercurrent in his earlier conversation with the colonel and the governor that suggested he had no choice in the matter, although it had never been stated outright. Now he realized that to get him to comply, they would only have to send a telegram to have him placed under the colonel's direct command; then, if he declined to accept the task voluntarily, he could be ordered to do so.

On a height overlooking the town, the carriage turned off Pecos Road at the drive leading to a large Spanish colonial house with gleaming white stucco walls and a red tile roof. At the imposing entrance, Vince and the colonel were greeted by the governor and his attractive wife, Martha Sheldon. She led the way into the luxuriously furnished parlor, where they waited for the Carranzas to arrive.

"My husband was positively radiant with happiness when he came home today," Mrs. Sheldon said to Vince, placing a hand on his arm. "He said he's found the very man he needed."

"I hope that proves to be the case, ma'am," Vince replied, and just then the governor entered with the grandee. Leaning on a cane, Don Raimundo was bowed and wizened with age, and his face was deeply wrinkled, but his eyes were as keenly alert as those of a youth.

It was easy to believe that the grandee stood near the throne of Spain, for he had a compelling air of authority about him. But he was also genuinely amiable, and he looked eagerly at Vince as the two were introduced. "It is a great pleasure indeed to meet you, Captain Bolton," he said in his crisp Castilian, shaking hands with a surprisingly firm grip.

"The pleasure and honor are mine, Excellency," Vince replied in fluent Spanish.

"No, no, you must call me Don Raimundo. There is no need for such formality between us, my friend. Come, let us sit down. I have been looking forward to talking with you."

Immediately liking the gracious, dignified man, Vince sat beside him on a couch, and they began to discuss the journey. More reluctant than ever to take the elderly man into a situation likely to be perilous, Vince set about trying to dissuade him from it.

The grandee quickly interrupted with a question. "Have you not agreed to be our guide, Captain Bolton?" he asked with disappointment.

"I'm not sure you completely understand what your intentions entail, Don Raimundo. It will be a journey with such hardships and dangers that your life will be in serious peril."

The old man nodded and seemed to be thinking for a moment. Then he approached the subject from a different angle. "Are you a religious man, Captain Bolton?"

Vince smiled. "Few soldiers who have been in combat aren't at least moderately religious."

Don Raimundo laughed in agreement. "Yes, few indeed. I, Captain, am deeply religious. Long ago a relative of mine was martyred while in service to God, and so brought great honor to my family. But in return my family has allowed his remains to lie in a wilderness, which is a disgrace. After devoting most of my life to my country, I am now in a position to correct that shameful neglect. It is something I must do."

Vince, too, had risked his life for a cause—and would continue to do so—so he understood the grandee's feelings. "Very well, sir. I'll be your guide, and I'll do my best to make the journey successful and safe. But I believe you should reconsider taking your daughter along, Don Raimundo. It will be an extremely difficult journey for a woman."

The old grandee nodded his head for a moment.

Then, with deliberation, he said, "I've read extensively about women who live here in the wilderness, under circumstances as arduous as this journey will be."

"Their situation is different. For many generations, while the frontier in this country was moving westward, women have lived in the wilderness. The skills and knowledge for dealing with those circumstances have been passed down from mother to daughter."

Smiling whimsically, the old man shrugged. "I would rather Arabella had stayed in Spain, for her own safety, but she is determined to be by my side on this trip. If you would like, you are welcome to try to dissuade her," the grandee said with a chuckle. "Believe me, I have tried. But she has a strong will, and a stronger body. I am sure she can endure the journey."

The grandee's mind was obviously made up. Vince began to wonder what this woman was like.

When he mentioned the trouble from outlaws that the legend of the Gran Quivira treasure could create, the old man replied that the contacts between his party and others had been very limited. "The only ones who should know of our destination are officials, such as the governor. I will ask my daughter to question the servants to make certain they have talked to no one, and she will warn them to keep silent about our destination."

"Very well, Don Raimundo," Vince said with resignation. His last hope of averting the dangerous and probably fruitless mission had been squelched, and now he would have to put all his energy into trying to make it a success, though the odds against it were considerable. Vince was disappointed, too, that he would not be in Socorro to stop Big Jim Congor from doing more harm.

But he had been given a goal, and he would do his best to reach it.

Turning to the grandee, he said, "The place we're to search, Chupadera Mesa, is fairly large. Is it possible to identify the part of the mesa Padre Eusebio went to for meditation?"

"Perhaps," Don Raimundo replied, pondering. "The letters are very old and difficult to read, of course. Arabella went through them and . . ." He broke off, turning to the door. "Ah, here she is now. She can tell you about the letters herself."

Looking toward the door, Vince had to conceal his surprise as he got his first look at Arabella. About twenty years old, she was tall and slender, the most strikingly attractive woman he had ever seen. Her delicate, aristocratic features were perfectly sculpted, and the faintest tinge of pink colored her smooth, alabaster cheeks. The thick tresses of blue-black hair arranged on top of her head and her large, dark eyes made an arresting contrast to her milky white skin.

Wearing a gown of emerald brocade with ivory lace at the wrists and throat, Arabella was trying to understand something Martha Sheldon was saying in her limited Spanish as they stepped into the room. Then the young woman turned and looked at Vince. As their eyes met, a subtle communication as tangible as a physical contact passed between them. It was an intense mutual attraction, completely unlike anything he had ever experienced.

A blush that began stealing up Arabella's slender throat to her cheeks revealed a fleeting instant of confusion, and then she collected herself. Lifting her chin, she was perfectly composed as she crossed the room to meet Vince. Her father introduced them, and Vince noticed the alluring scent of her perfume as he bowed over her soft, cool hand.

He could see that the grandee and his daughter had a close relationship as the man smiled at her affectionately. He also seemed fond of teasing her, for he said, "I regret to tell you, my dear, that the captain has expressed strong misgivings about your accompanying me to Gran Quivira."

Arabella lifted her eyebrows. "Indeed? And for what reason, Captain?"

Vince saw in Arabella's directness the strong will that

her father had just described. "Because of the danger," he replied.

"Then you can put your mind at rest. If the journey is not too dangerous for you, it certainly will not be too dangerous for me."

Vince was again impressed by the woman's spirit and saw that it would probably be impossible to talk her out of anything. "Be that as it may, the issue has been settled in your favor, Señorita Arabella. Don Raimundo has insisted that you go."

"Naturally," she said, smiling at her father. "One of his greatest enjoyments is scolding me, and he would find the journey tedious without that pleasure to while away the time."

Vince and the grandee laughed heartily as Arabella took a seat. Joining her, the two men asked about the information in the priest's letters. Briefly she described it and then suggested that Vince come to their house the following morning and read what she had copied from the letters. He quickly agreed to do so.

The conversation continued as a maid brought in a tray of aperitifs and served them. Hamilton and the Sheldons understood Spanish sufficiently to know that Vince had committed himself to act as guide for the party; deeply satisfied, the three of them talked among themselves as Vince discussed preparations for the journey with the Carranzas.

Because his knowledge of New Mexico Territory was limited, Don Raimundo had assumed that the trek toward Gran Quivira would begin from Santa Fe, but Vince pointed out that Socorro was a more logical jumping-off point. It was much closer to Gran Quivira, with a road of sorts part of the way.

"The road crosses the Los Piños Mountains, east of Socorro," he explained. "It ends on the eastern side of the mountains, and Gran Quivira is still a good distance east of there, though beyond the mountains the terrain is low hills and broken flatlands, so it's possible to get wagons across it."

"Very well. We will go to Socorro," Don Raimundo said, lifting his arms in conclusion. "We brought much more baggage from Spain than we will need there and on the journey, of course."

"Yes, but I suggest you move all of your belongings to Socorro. The hotel there isn't suitable, but my father is manager of the stagecoach way station, which has ample accommodations for you and your servants while we're preparing to set out for Gran Quivira. We can hire a dray from a freight company to take your excess baggage there, and my father will look after it."

Don Raimundo gave Vince a broad smile and, taking his hand, said, "Your kindness warms my heart, Captain Bolton. I am most grateful to you and your gracious father."

A moment later the maid stepped in and announced that dinner was served. Don Raimundo and Martha Sheldon led the way into the large, elegant dining room, and the governor escorted Arabella as Vince and Hamilton followed.

The meal was delicious, but Vince scarcely tasted the food, for Arabella claimed his full attention. In the soft glow of the candelabra, she was bewitching, and her vivacious personality brought a vibrance to the gathering.

During conversation over dinner, Vince learned how Don Raimundo had come to have such a young daughter at his advanced age. He had married a second time in his later years, and Arabella was the only child from that marriage. Vince also learned that she was well educated and had made all the financial arrangements for their trip from Spain. He listened eagerly as Don Raimundo told him of his daughter's spirited personality.

"My three sons from my first marriage were young men when she was born, and they adore her," Don Raimundo said, smiling at her fondly. "They taught Arabella to be an expert shot with firearms and a fearless rider. But, while they made her much too willful, she is also an entertaining companion."

Arabella quickly spoke up to deny that she was willful; then she broke off as she realized that by bluntly contradicting him, she was proving her father right.

As the old man laughed, Vince reflected that her headstrong nature might create problems on the trip. Nevertheless, he suddenly realized that because of her, he was now anticipating with pleasure the many weeks ahead the trip and its preparations would occupy. Glancing at her, the captain was startled that she was looking at him, and she flashed him a smile that dazzled him with its directness.

When dinner was finished, everyone returned to the parlor. Presently, Don Raimundo and Arabella thanked the Sheldons for their hospitality and made their farewells. After they were gone, Vince talked with the governor for a few minutes, filling him in on the discussion with the Carranzas. Then he and Hamilton left.

After the carriage had taken him back to the garrison, Vince walked about the quadrangle for a time, too restless to sleep. It was the most beautiful evening he could remember, silent except for the sounds of the chirping crickets and the sighing of the cool breeze through the trees, while overhead a canopy of brilliant stars lit the velvety sky.

He could not recall having been so attuned before to the beauty around him. The army had been the focus of his life until now, and all of his attention and energy had been consumed by it. But he knew that had changed abruptly and forever the moment he had met Arabella.

Chapter Three

At midmorning the next day, Vince arrived at the luxurious house the Carranzas had rented for their stay in Santa Fe. Arabella met him at the door, dismissing the maid who had come to answer the knock. She was just as lovely as the evening before, the fitted bodice of her yellow, summery dress defining the curves of her slender body. Hanging loose, her long, thick hair reflected glints of sunlight.

As she returned his greeting, her large, dark eyes sparkled with pleasure at seeing him again. Then she pointed apologetically to the vast, somewhat spartan entry hall. "I trust you will overlook our surroundings, Captain Bolton," she said. "As you know, our residence here is temporary, and we are not prepared to receive guests properly."

Vince followed her in and peered around at the hall. "It appears very comfortable to me, Señorita Arabella. And I hope I'm not being too bold in saying that in time I wish to be more of a family friend than merely a guest."

Pursing her lips to control the quick smile that made her beautiful face radiant, she nodded. "My father regards you very highly, so you are already a family friend, Captain Bolton."

"Then you should address me by my given name, which is Vincent."

"So I shall, and you must call me simply Arabella.

Come, Vincent, let us go into the parlor, and I will show you my notes on the information from Padre Eusebio's letters. My father is resting now, but you and I can discuss any further details about the journey."

As they entered the parlor, a man emerged from another door. He stopped, looked curiously at Vince, and waited for Arabella to introduce them. The man was Federico Murillo, the functionary from the Spanish foreign ministry who accompanied the Carranzas as interpreter and attended to business with public officials. Wearing the dark business suit of his profession, Murillo was a small man with thick, swarthy features, and a scowl of vague dissatisfaction seemed to be engraved on his face.

After Arabella had made the introductions, Murillo murmured with a bow, "I am pleased to meet you, Captain Bolton." Turning to the young woman, he asked, "Where might I find your father, Señorita Arabella?"

"My father is resting in his room, Señor Murillo, and does not wish to be disturbed. Is there anything with which I might be of help?"

Murillo shook his head quickly, and then bidding Vince good day, he disappeared down the hall toward the rear of the house.

As Vince and Arabella went into the parlor, she said, "Murillo never lets my father out of his sight for too long. My father considers the man an inconvenience."

"Why did your father bring him along, then?" Vince asked.

"Because he was designated by the government to accompany my father. As one of His Majesty's most trusted friends and counselors, my father can never travel to a foreign nation as a private citizen."

"Couldn't he have asked for someone more personable?"

Sounding as if she were repeating remarks her father had made, she replied, "Statecraft is the art of compromise to achieve consensus. My father needed a foreign ministry official, not a friend."

Thinking with wry amusement that he could never be a politician, Vince nodded and dropped the subject.

Arabella opened a drawer in the sideboard, took out the extracts she had made from the priest's letters, and handed the sheets of paper to Vince. After they had taken seats on a couch, he looked through the notes, translating her small, neat handwriting. The priest's description of his place of meditation made it apparent that it was located at Chupadera Mesa. Two of the extracts suggested that it could have been some sort of shelter on the north rim of the mesa.

Thanking her, Vince handed the notes back and said they would be helpful. Then they discussed plans for the trip to Socorro. Three freight wagons would be needed to transport supplies for Don Raimundo, Arabella, and their servants, and arrangements had been made at the local stage office for a coach for Don Raimundo. The trip would take several days, with frequent stops to avoid fatiguing the grandee. The Spaniards would leave in two days, and Vince would catch up with them later, after he had seen to the cavalry escort and their supplies.

When he learned that Arabella would ride her saddle horse during the journey, Vince was impressed. The beautiful young woman was far more resourceful than he would have thought. As they parted, planning to meet again outside of Socorro, Vince thought of the many ways she had surprised and delighted him, and he wondered what their next meeting would bring.

In the days that followed, Captain Vince Bolton was swept up in a swirl of activity in preparation for the long trip. First he equipped the Carranzas and their large party, arranging the purchase of the three freight wagons they would need to transport their possessions. He had known the Carranzas were wealthy people who traveled in style, but when he saw how many things

they considered necessities and required to have with
them, he realized that this was shaping up to be an
expedition rather than a journey. They could well af-
ford to hire drivers for the wagons from the local stage
line, he decided.

The next step was to acquire the horses for the journey. Getting the wagons across the mountains would
require double teams, he figured, and the stagecoach in
which Don Raimundo would ride needed three teams.
Also, there should be a remuda of spare horses in the
event any of the teams went lame.

In addition to wagons and horses, Vince saw that
enough food and water were purchased and loaded,
and he mapped out an itinerary with the hired drivers
that would not tax Don Raimundo. By traveling about
thirty miles each day, the party would reach Socorro in
four to five days, stopping outside of towns beside the
Rio Grande at night. Vince instructed the sergeant and
half of the twenty men who would accompany the party
to leave Santa Fe with them, with the other men and
Vince setting out two days later. He calculated that the
two groups would meet up on the last day of the journey.

Four days later, the captain and his men were twenty
miles outside of Socorro when they finally sighted Don
Raimundo's coach, with Murillo and some servants riding alongside. Vince left the wagons of supplies behind
and spurred his horse to a canter. He smiled in anticipation as he glimpsed Arabella through the trees.

Wearing a stylish riding costume of heavy blue serge
and a wide hat trimmed with pale blue ribbon, she was
a vision of beauty. Her horse, a magnificent Arab gelding, was decked out with a saddle and bridle that were
lavishly decorated in silver and gold. The gelding was
frisky, but Arabella was an expert rider and controlled it
effortlessly.

The column stopped when Vince approached and
greeted Arabella and her father, who climbed down
from the stagecoach upon seeing the captain. Vince

remarked on Arabella's expert riding skills, and Don
Raimundo smiled and said, "She takes after her father
in many ways." Then he continued, "During the journey, Arabella and I would consider it an honor and a
pleasure if you would share our meals with us, Captain.
The cook will not have time to prepare a hot meal this
evening, but she will be able to provide a satisfactory
dinner from the provisions we have."

Somewhat surprised by the invitation, Vince was also
deeply pleased. Thanking the grandee, he accepted it
and asked how their journey had been thus far. Don
Raimundo replied that it had been comfortable in the
coach, but Arabella interrupted to tell the captain that
her father was tiring.

"May we stop here for the night, Vincent?" she said in
her melodic voice. "My father would benefit from the
extra hours of rest."

"My daughter!" Don Raimundo exclaimed. "She worries more about my well-being than her own."

"Your daughter is right," Vince said. "This is a good
spot to camp, and we all could use a rest. I'll give orders
for the soldiers to set up camp."

An hour later, when the maid served the meal, Vince,
Arabella, and Don Raimundo sat around a small campfire. Several loaves of bread had been sliced, and there
were earthenware pots of caviar and paté, along with a
variety of spicy sausages and several kinds of cheese.
The cook had also filled bowls with pickles, condiments,
and sliced fruit, and a bottle of aged red wine accompanied the meal.

A short time after dinner was finished, Arabella had
the servants prepare her father's bed, which was in one
of the wagons, as they had done the previous nights.
Vince assisted the elderly man into the canvas-covered
wagon while Arabella went into a tent the servants had
erected for her. As the rest of the party settled into their
bedrolls for the night, Vince spread his blankets beside
the fire.

In the early morning darkness before dawn, Vince

awoke as the cook began building up the fire. He brought buckets of water from the creek for her and then shaved and dusted his uniform as the camp stirred to life. The servants bustled about, Arabella's maid taking hot water into her tent and Don Raimundo's valet assisting him. The drivers gulped down coffee and tortillas and then harnessed the horses.

As the sun peeked above the horizon, the party rode out, with Vince and Arabella at the front of the column on horseback and the coach and wagons falling into line behind them. They intended to reach Socorro before evening.

When the horses had settled down to a steady, comfortable gait, Vince and Arabella began to talk. She had made a few references to her life in Spain that puzzled him, and he wanted to know more about her. While he looked forward to many happy hours with her in the weeks to come, he had also begun to think about the time that lay beyond those weeks. Would she and her father return to Spain, never to see him again? His life seemed so much more complete with her a part of it, and he wondered if she felt the same.

The prospects he had been considering received a chill blast as she talked about the journey. "For years, we have discussed the necessity of having our relative's remains interred in holy ground," she said, "but the opportunity for this journey came at a good time. A man has asked for my hand in marriage, and this trip will provide ample time and opportunity for my father and me to consider it."

Feeling her words like a physical blow, Vince knew he should have foreseen what she had just told him; with her incomparable beauty and family background, she had to have a host of suitors in Spain. "Only one?" he asked, smiling to cover his feelings. "I thought you would have at least as many proposals of marriage as you do invitations to social events."

She laughed and shrugged, acknowledging that there had been others. "Only one that is due serious consider-

ation, however. He is Eduardo Alejandro Serraño y
Carbella, Duke de Valencia. My father and I agreed to
consider his proposal during our journey and inform
him of our decision upon our return."

"Have you known him long?" Vince asked.

"I have met him two or three times." She noticed
Vince's surprised expression. "It would not be a marriage of love, Vincent. There are other considerations,
such as family line and wealth."

"Does that bother you, Arabella?"

She looked far ahead of them toward the horizon. "I
must do what is right for my family and my country."
After a long pause, she turned to the captain and said in
a lively tone, "Now, tell me about your lady love, Vincent."

He let out a laugh and replied, "I have no one."

"Come, Vincent! I have told you very personal information about myself, so you must do the same. There
must be someone."

"No, there is no one. I am married to the army, Arabella."

She studied him musingly and then with a sly smile
commented, "I should think you would want a better
partner than the army, Vincent."

Feeling a bit uncomfortable under her scrutiny,
Vince tried to divert her attention to another subject.
Pointing to a grove of piñon trees, he said, "Have you
eaten any of the nuts from those trees? They are tender
and delicately flavored."

Arabella smiled as if knowing perfectly well his intent
in changing the subject. "My father and I have been
told about them, but we have not yet sampled one."

"My father sometimes uses them in stews," Vince
explained. "Perhaps he will have some on hand when
we arrive at the way station."

"I am eager to meet your father, Vincent. He must be
a remarkable man to have raised a son like you." Before
he could answer, Arabella spurred her horse forward,
leaving him behind in its dust.

Vince shook his head. She was quite an amazing woman, and so breathtakingly beautiful. But he was dejected over the news that she was seriously considering marriage, one that would have social, financial, and political implications. He knew he could never compete on those grounds, and that made the duke a formidable opponent.

At sunset Vince and Arabella led the column into the way station compound, the vehicles rumbling through the gate and stirring up a cloud of dust. As Vince helped Arabella down from her horse, Harvey Bolton emerged from the office, looking with bewilderment at the huge party accompanying his son.

Giving Vince a hug, he said, "Just what is going on, son? You've got enough people here to start your own town."

"I'll explain later, Dad. But first I'd like you to meet someone." Ushering his father over to the stagecoach, where Arabella was about to see to the grandee, he said, "Arabella, this is Harvey Bolton, my father. And Dad, this is Señorita Arabella Christina Albara y Carranza."

Speaking fluent Spanish, the elder Bolton bowed over Arabella's hand and greeted her. Then Vince assisted Don Raimundo from the coach and introduced him and Murillo to his father.

"We'll all be staying for several days, Dad. The soldiers and drivers are equipped to camp out, but if you don't mind, I'd like for the rest of us to have rooms."

"That can be arranged with no trouble, son, provided a few of the servants don't mind doubling up."

Don Raimundo stepped forward and said in a shaky voice, "We are most grateful for your generous hospitality, Señor Bolton. Your son has been a most gracious and knowledgeable guide, and we are fortunate to have found him."

Arabella took the grandee's arm. "Are you all right, Father? You sound rather weary." Looking at Harvey, she continued, "I think we had better get to bed right away, Señor Bolton. If you don't mind, we'll talk with you in the morning."

"But you haven't had dinner yet," Vince observed.

"Oh, Vincent. You should know as well as anyone how many provisions we have with us. It will not take our cook long to prepare a light meal before we retire. Surely you do not think we expect your generous father to have a meal for this many people ready with no notice!"

Harvey gave a laugh and said, "No, I don't have dinner ready, but you can rest assured, young lady, that you will have a good, hearty breakfast tomorrow morning."

After Harvey had escorted the party to their quarters, showing the servants to their rooms and bidding Arabella, her father, and Murillo good night, he and Vince went to the way station office. There, Harvey poured cups of coffee from a fire-blackened pot and said to his son, "Now are you going to tell me what on earth is going on?"

Vince laughed. Taking a sip of coffee, he briefly explained what the Carranzas hoped to do. "But we can't let word get out that we're going to Gran Quivira," he cautioned. "If outlaws got wind of it, they would figure that Don Raimundo knows something about the treasure that was supposed to be there at one time."

"That's true," his father agreed. "Well, no one will hear it from me. You know, I never thought I'd ever see a woman anywhere near as pretty as your mother was. But I'll have to admit that Arabella comes fairly close."

"Yes," Vince said, leaning back in his chair. "She's extremely attractive, with a personality that matches. She's also considering a marriage proposal from a very well-placed man in Spain, the Duke of Valencia."

"Oh . . . a duke, eh?" Harvey stretched his arms and clasped his hands behind his head. Then, with a twinkle in his eye, he added, "Well, just remember, son. He's in Spain with his hankering to marry her, but you're here with her, aren't you?"

Chapter Four

Upstairs in the Sundowner Saloon in Socorro, Big Jim Congor was sleeping soundly in his room the next morning when a voice speaking softly but insistently awakened him. Slowly he opened his heavy eyes. The figure quietly calling his name was his second-in-command, a weasel-faced man from St. Louis named Lew Frable, who among other things was a supremely skilled pickpocket. Congor growled at the man, "What do you want?"

"Somethin' you'll wanna know about is goin' on, Big Jim. I wouldn't have woke you up, but I knew you'd want me to."

Congor lifted his head and looked at the clock on the nightstand. "It's only eight o'clock!" he barked. "What do you mean waking me up at this time of the morning?"

"Important things are goin' on, Big Jim," Frable replied, an anxious grin on his sharp, pointed face. "I know you haven't slept very long, but there's somethin' you'll want to know about."

"It'd better be important!" Congor snarled threateningly. "Get me some coffee up here from the saloon!"

"I already did that, Big Jim. There's a whole pot of it, strong and hot, waitin' for you in the other room."

Grumbling resentfully, Congor threw the covers back and sat up on the edge of the bed. He also uncovered the slender body of a young woman, lying with her

39

back to him. Rosa Montero's weeping had kept him awake far into the night until he had slapped her into silence. As she reached back and fumbled for the covers to pull over herself, Frable snickered and leered at her avidly.

"If you want to see her, you can look at her in the hotel—after you pay for her," Congor growled. "Go pour me some coffee."

Frable rushed out, and Congor heaved his massive bulk to a standing position and pushed his feet into his slippers. Always out of sorts upon arising, he felt weary and even more irritable from lack of sleep. He picked up his robe from a chair and put it on as he went into the sitting room.

His yellow teeth bared in an ingratiating grin, Frable handed Congor a cup of coffee. Taking it, Congor went to the liquor cabinet and added a splash of whiskey; then he sat down heavily in his chair and took a sip. "Now what is so important that I can't get any sleep?"

"It's that soldier, Bolton. He's back. He got back late last night and brought some Spaniards with him."

His anger swelling, Congor's hand trembled as he took a deep drink of coffee. The problem that Vince Bolton represented had seemed to be solved when he left, but now it was back again. A problem that was too dangerous to ignore, it was also one with no satisfactory solution that he had been able to find.

"Spaniards?" Congor growled. "Who are they, and what's he doing with them?"

"I don't know, Big Jim. At first I thought they was Mexicans, but rumor has it they're from Spain."

Congor took another drink of coffee and nodded. "All right. Send for the barber down the street. And see that Rosa gets back to the hotel soon. There might be an early customer for her. I'll be downstairs in about an hour."

While waiting for the barber, Congor pondered the situation morosely. Years before, he had been in the army, but the regimentation and discipline had been unbearable. He had deserted about a week after enlisting, and ever since then, he had detested the very sight of an army uniform. When he had first met up with Bolton, everything about the man infuriated Congor. His uniform was immaculately neat, his knee boots gleamed, and his campaign hat was set at a precise angle. Tall and straight, the captain towered over others, and his tanned, handsome features were set in the firm line of one who never wavers. He epitomized authority, Congor's great enemy in life.

Congor knew he had used poor judgment when he had chosen to send two men after Bolton that night in Socorro to teach him a lesson. They had been no match for the captain. Afterward, when Bolton had confronted him in the saloon in front of his men, Congor had lost some of his power over them. Bolton's challenging him without any retribution had left the door wide open for others to follow suit.

When Bolton had disappeared, Congor had hoped that he had been recalled to his regiment or had been posted elsewhere—anything to get him out of Socorro. Since no one would expect Congor to retaliate against a man who was many miles away, the problem would have been eliminated, and in time Bolton's challenge would have been forgotten. Now that Bolton was back, everyone would be waiting to see what happened.

The barber tapped on the door and then came in with a basin of hot water, towels, and other paraphernalia. Sitting back in his chair as the barber put steaming towels on his face and shaved him, Congor continued pondering his problem with Bolton. Having him killed by a shotgun blast from a dark alley was one option, but a perilously dangerous one. The attempt could fail, with disastrous consequences, since Bolton was such a formidable opponent. If it succeeded, Congor knew he would be immediately suspected of being behind it. That could result in an investigation by the army or by territorial authorities who would, at the very least, discover and destroy what he had built up in Socorro.

Despite his train of thought, Congor felt better after having the shave, as he always did. When the barber was gone, he chose a satisfactorily colorful suit and dressed. Although the problem with Bolton was a dilemma, it could still resolve itself; the captain might leave again shortly and never return, or something else could happen. In a much better frame of mind, Congor left his rooms.

His mood improved even more as he went downstairs to the saloon, where he could bask in the power he had over others. At this early hour, few people other than his men were there, standing at the bar and scattered among the tables.

When Lew Frable saw him, he grinned widely. "Well, here's Big Jim, lookin' mighty spruce."

Congor nodded benignly to him and others in reply to their greetings. Some of the men worked for him because of indebtedness or some other hold he had over them, and Congor thought that a few of those men spoke less heartily this morning. It was a very few, but enough to make Congor feel that he should demonstrate his authority. Several of the customers were men who had been waiting to see him, and Frable sent them over, one at a time.

Antonio Montero was the first to step up to the table. He was a few inches taller than his brother, Juan, but they shared the same dark features and swarthy skin. Already starting in on his daily intake of beer, Antonio set down his glass and said, "Big Jim, I need to talk to you." He cleared his throat nervously when Congor looked up at him. "I want to work out some way to get my girl, Rosa, out of the hotel. I'm the one who owes you money, not her. It . . . it's not right for her to have to be there."

Congor smiled, thinking of Rosa Montero's supple young form. She was proving to be worth her while in the hotel and in Congor's bed. Her father, standing before him, was clearly terrified, his voice quaking as he trembled, and Congor saw this as an opportunity to reclaim the power that Bolton had stripped from him. The prospect of doing that further improved Congor's disposition.

"Well, we can certainly talk about it," Congor said cheerfully. "Let's go up to my rooms."

As the small man followed him up the stairs, Congor pondered what means to use in making an example of Antonio Montero. Among the weapons his bulk allowed him to carry undetected was a derringer, but he decided upon his stiletto as less noisy and more satisfying.

Once they were in the upstairs hall, Congor suddenly turned and gripped Montero by the throat, slamming him against the wall. "You want your little Rosa out of the hotel, Montero? Well, you needn't do anything more. She is out of the hotel—and in my bed!" His frustrated rage fueling his strength, Congor dug his fingers into the man's throat, holding him firmly against the wall. The only sound Montero could utter was a breathless wheeze as he tugged vainly at Congor's hand. Taking out his stiletto, Congor held it in front of Montero's face to give him a good look at it, then lowered it slowly to his chest.

His eyes glazed in panic, Montero struggled frantically. Congor put the tip of the knife against the man's chest, over his heart, and then pushed very slowly. The tip penetrated Montero's clothes, then his flesh. When the blade touched bone and began grating through it, the man's limbs thrashed wildly as his hoarse, ragged gasps filled the hall.

When the tip of the blade reached his heart, Antonio Montero's movements turned into death throes. A moment later he was motionless, sagging against the wall. Congor pulled the blade out, wiped it on the dead man's shirt, and then put it away as he stepped back to the stairs.

Congor shouted down the stairs for Frable, who ran up within seconds. Pointing to the body, the big man snarled, "Have somebody get rid of it." He turned to go down the stairs but then halted. Looking back at Frable, he added, "After you get rid of the body, I want to talk to you." Smiling with grim satisfaction, Congor continued down the stairs.

As Frable knelt down to lift Antonio Montero's body, the tearstained face of Rosa Montero peered out from around the corner of Congor's door. She watched in silent horror as her father's bloodied body was dragged off toward the back staircase. The tears that flowed down her face mixed with her rage, and she swore that Big Jim Congor would be held responsible for this act.

Once Big Jim Congor had returned to the saloon and resumed his seat, he felt calm, refreshed, and better able to deal with the problem that Vince Bolton represented. Frable came down and joined him fifteen minutes later, and Congor questioned him about the Spaniards.

Frable knew their family name and that there were a nobleman, his daughter, many servants, and nearly two dozen soldiers with them, but other than that, he knew little. They had come to Socorro from Santa Fe and were staying at the stagecoach way station.

Congor grunted. "The way station, huh? Don't you have a friend who works there?"

"Jake Clinton. He's not really a friend, but I do know him. Likes to drink."

"Then why don't you buy him a few, Lew? He should know plenty about the Spaniards. See if you can loosen his tongue about them."

"Oh . . . *I* see what you're gettin' at," Frable mused. "I'll be able to get somethin' out of him. Don't worry."

Congor rose up from his chair with effort, saying, "Give him all the drinks he can hold and take him to the hotel for free. Let him know that the more he finds out and tells you, the more he'll get of what he wants, on the house. You can also give him a few dollars."

Congor dismissed Frable, pondering the plan that was taking shape in his mind. It was obvious that Bolton had been designated as an official adviser or escort for the Spaniards, and that was the key to the plan. Now he merely needed to find out why the Spaniards had come all the way from their native country to Socorro. Once he knew that, he would quietly arrange circumstances that would thwart them— and place Captain Vince Bolton in the worst possible light.

The next morning, having again arisen much earlier than usual, Congor was disgruntled. After plying Jake Clinton with drinks until late at night and taking him to the hotel, Lew Frable had learned very little. There were rumors that more soldiers were arriving to escort the Spaniards and that Vince Bolton was planning a long journey. But as far as the purpose of the Spaniards' trip, Clinton had known only that it had something to do with a priest who had died.

"Clinton promised to see if he could find out any more today," Frable said, "and he's gonna meet me tonight for more free drinks."

Nodding absently, Congor suddenly realized that the scarcity of information was in itself very revealing. It meant that whatever the Spaniards intended to do was being kept secret. The purpose therefore was important and could be obstructed if the information became known. Congor knew he had to find out that purpose.

The most reliable way of doing that occurred to him in a flash, and instinctively he decided to keep his plan to himself. "Have my buggy brought around to the alley," he ordered Frable. "I may be gone for as long as a week, so keep things in hand here."

Frable assured his boss that he would keep everything in order.

When Frable had left, Congor quickly packed a bag with clothes and other necessities for his trip. He was going to Santa Fe, where the Spaniards had stayed before coming to Socorro. Surely, Congor reasoned, someone there was bound to know what those people hoped to gain.

* * *

Standing in Socorro's general store, Vince Bolton glanced over his list of necessities for the journey. "That seems to be everything that I need, Mr. Killian," he said to the owner.

"Well, it's plenty, and I appreciate the business, Captain Bolton," Killian replied with satisfaction, looking over the list he had made as Vince named off items. "How soon do you need all this?"

"I'd like to have it within the next day or two, if possible."

"I can make it sooner than that, Captain Bolton. I'll load it into a wagon and bring it to the way station after I close the store tonight."

Vince nodded, and after shaking hands with the man, he left the store. As he crossed the boardwalk to his horse at the hitch rail, he saw Juan Montero riding down the street, a moody frown on his face. The man's frown changed to a wan smile as he saw Vince, and he waved in reply as the captain called out to him.

Mounting his horse, Vince rode down the street and reined up beside Juan. They exchanged greetings, and when Vince asked how things were going for him, Montero hesitated. Then he sighed heavily and shrugged. "I have the same problem that has troubled me for years, Vincent," he replied morosely. "It is my brother, Antonio."

"What's he been up to now?"

"Pilar, his wife, came to my ranch this morning and told me that he left early yesterday morning and did not come home last night."

Vince pushed back his hat and rubbed his forehead. "Has Antonio done this sort of thing before?"

Juan sighed again, shaking his head. "No, never. He's stayed away from home until late in the night sometimes, but never this long before."

"Considering who he's involved with," Vince mused, "it's reasonable to think that something bad may have happened to him. Have you been to the Sundowner to ask about him?"

"No, and I do not intend to go there," Juan replied firmly. "I have my own family to think about, Vincent, and I am not going to get into any trouble with Big Jim Congor. If Antonio has had some trouble with him or his men, it has nothing to do with me."

"Well, if you like, I'll go there and ask about him," Vince said, "but I won't mention you or this conversation. I've known Antonio and Pilar for years, and I'll just say that I want to know where he is because Pilar is without money and has no food in the house."

Juan smiled gratefully. "That is very good of you, Vincent. Antonio is still my brother, and I am concerned about him. But please be careful. I don't want you to be involved in any trouble over this."

The captain's blue eyes sparkled as he said, "If there's trouble, it'll be because Congor and his men start it, and dealing with it will be a pleasure, Juan. I'm expected back at the way station shortly, so I'll go there first to check in. Then I'll go to the Sundowner to see what I can find out about Antonio."

Juan earnestly thanked Vince again and then rode away as the captain turned his horse toward the way station. When he rode into the way station compound a short time later, he saw two other horses tethered beside his father's gelding in front of the office. One was Marshal Buell's pinto, and the other was a roan that belonged to Ira Chapman, a young man who worked part-time for the marshal as a deputy and jailor.

After exchanging greetings with the marshal and deputy, Vince sat down and talked to them for a few minutes and then stood up to leave. "If you gents will excuse me, there's something I need to check into at the Sundowner."

"The Sundowner?" Buell echoed. "Have you had another run-in with Congor, Vince?"

The captain shook his head, and after briefly explaining about Antonio, he turned toward the door. "I should be back in plenty of time for dinner," he added to his father.

"Well, me and Ira here will mosey over that way with you, Vince," the marshal announced. "Come on, Ira."

"I'll go, too," Harvey put in, wincing as he pushed himself to his feet. "I need to stir around and loosen up this bad leg of mine."

"Now wait a minute," Vince objected. "I don't need an escort to go over to the Sundowner."

"We know that, Vince." Buell chuckled, and the others laughed and nodded in agreement. "And you ain't getting an escort. It's been a day or two since I've been there, and I like for Congor to remember that I'm around. Besides, I'm kind of interested myself in finding out about Antonio Montero."

Vince nodded and shrugged, and then he put on his hat and followed the others as they filed out the door.

After mounting up, the four men rode away from the way station and through the town to the Sundowner Saloon. They tied their horses to the hitch rail outside and entered the saloon to see only a few customers seated at the tables and along the bar during the early afternoon hour. Vince glanced around and spotted half a dozen of Congor's men, but Antonio Montero was not among them.

The bartender, as though anticipating trouble, frowned warily as he swabbed the bar in front of Vince and the others. "What'll it be?" he growled.

"Nothing," Vince replied curtly. "I'm looking for Antonio Montero."

The bartender hesitated, his eyes reflecting caution as he glanced from Vince to the marshal and back. Then he shrugged and shook his head. "I ain't seen Montero. He might have left town."

"Why would he leave town?" Vince asked.

"I didn't say he had. I said he might have. All I know is that I ain't seen him today." The bartender started wiping the bar, clearly uninterested in continuing the conversation.

Vince turned and looked at Congor's men, then asked, "Do any of you know where Montero is?"

None of the men replied, and each one turned away as Vince looked at him. One of them, leaning back on the rear legs of a chair with his feet propped on a table, lifted his lips in a silent sneer. Vince covered the distance with two long steps and then hooked a foot under a front leg on the chair and tugged. The man spat a stream of surprised oaths as he sprawled on the floor with a crash, the back of the chair splintering.

Gripping the front of the man's shirt, Vince jerked him to his feet. "I asked if you know where Montero is," he grated.

The man shrank back apprehensively, shaking his head and stuttering that he knew nothing about Montero. Vince pushed the man away and stepped back to the bar.

The bartender glared at the marshal, and pointing to Vince, he demanded, "Ain't you gonna do anything about that, Marshal? He's trying to start trouble, and he broke one of my chairs!"

"I don't see any trouble going on," Buell responded placidly. "The captain is just asking questions, and that galoot who fell on the chair was the one who broke it. Where's Congor? He should know something about Montero, since the man is in his debt."

"Big Jim ain't here," the bartender replied sullenly. "He's been out of town for the past few days."

"Well, how about the one who's in charge when Congor is gone?" the marshal persisted. "That's Frable, isn't it?"

"Yeah, but I don't know where he is," the bartender growled. "I ain't seen him since early this morning."

Turning to Vince, the marshal commented that coming to the saloon had apparently been a waste of time. Vince nodded in agreement, stood up, and walked toward the door with the lawmen and his father following. On the boardwalk outside, they conferred about what to do next. Going to Congor's hotel to ask about Antonio Montero seemed to be the best move, so they mounted up and rode on down the street.

As they approached the hotel, Ira Chapman pointed to the empty hitch rail in front of it. "The place usually doesn't open until evening," he said, "and they're probably sleeping now. If we get into a fracas here, I hope the bouncers don't wake up. One of them is a man I wouldn't want to have any trouble with. He's the size of a mountain."

"You seem to know a lot about this place, Ira," Buell commented, lifting his eyebrows and winking broadly at Vince and Harvey.

The young deputy flushed as Vince and the others laughed. They dismounted, and when the horses were tethered, the other men followed Vince as he stepped across the boardwalk and knocked on the door. Several minutes passed, during which Vince knocked again and again, and at last the door opened a crack.

A stout, ugly woman peered out sleepily, her angry frown disappearing as she looked at the auburn-haired captain, the marshal, and the others.

"We were told that Lew Frable was here. We'd like to see him," Vince told her.

The woman hesitated as she peered suspiciously at the men. Finally, she said in a shaky voice, "What do you want to see Mr. Frable about?"

"That's none of your business," the marshal put in curtly. "Now if you don't want me to clap you in jail for obstructing justice, you let us in there and tell the captain where Frable is."

"Well . . . all right," the woman said, reluctantly opening the door wider. "But be quiet. Just about everybody is sleeping now. Mr. Frable is upstairs in one of the private rooms."

Once the men had stepped inside, the woman closed and locked the door behind them. Vince followed her up the staircase, while his father and the lawmen waited in the dim, wide entry below.

Puffing and wheezing up the steps, the heavyset woman sighed and muttered worriedly, "I hope Mr. Congor won't be angry about all this."

Vince, intent only on finding out what he could about Antonio Montero, ignored the woman's whining. But once they were upstairs and going down a hall, the madam made a remark that drew his attention: "Mr. Congor told me to keep Rosa in a private room, so I don't know if Mr. Frable should—"

"Rosa Montero?" Vince snapped, interrupting her.

"Yes, that's right," the madam replied. "How did you know? Her room is on the left at the end of the hall. Mr. Congor wants her in a private room all by herself. He wants her to be . . ."

The woman's voice faded with surprise as Vince brushed past her and stepped rapidly toward the end of the hall. As he approached the door, he heard a muffled scream of distress coming from inside the room, followed by an angry snarl in a man's voice and the sharp sound of an open hand striking flesh. Gathering his strength, Vince hurled himself at the door.

As the flimsy lock gave way, the door slammed open with a loud crash. In the hall, the madam shrieked with alarm as she ran back toward the stairs at a lumbering pace.

Vince charged into the room and saw a small, weasel-faced man holding Rosa Montero down on the bed and slapping her as he struggled to undress her. Looking up at the tall captain with consternation, Lew Frable started to move back from the bed, but Vince stopped him by hurling his left fist into the man's stomach. Frable's breath burst from his lungs as he doubled over and stumbled backward. Vince took the opportunity to slam a right into Frable's face, the blow knocking the man back against the wall as blood burst from his mouth and nose. Frable slumped to the floor, unconscious.

Vince turned to the bed, where the young woman was straightening her disheveled clothes. "Rosa, I'm Vincent Bolton," he said. "Do you remember me?"

"Yes . . . yes, I remember you well, sir," she stammered as she rose from the bed. "God bless you for coming here, Captain Bolton. Please, I beg of you, take me away from this place, sir."

"That's exactly what I intend to do," he replied, putting an arm around her and leading her toward the door. "Come on, Rosa."

Sobbing with relief, the girl clung to him as he led her from the room. Walking back along the hall toward the stairs with her, Vince heard a growing uproar of shouting voices from the entry below. The madam was bellowing at the top of her voice, which was almost drowned out by men roaring at each other. From the top of the staircase, Vince looked down and saw that his father, Buell, and Ira were facing off with three bouncers.

One of the bouncers, a giant of a man, was obviously the one Ira Chapman had mentioned. Nearly seven feet tall, he was built like a gorilla and weighed well over three hundred pounds, every ounce of it solid bone and muscle. He appeared to be as stupid as he was large, looking in silence from one man to another, as though waiting for directions, while everyone else argued heatedly.

Vince and Rosa made their way down the stairs. On the first floor of the building, women were peeking out of the doors along the hall, and a fourth man was approaching from a back hallway. While the three bouncers were unarmed and wore only nightshirts, this man was fully clothed and wore a six-gun. Vince figured that he was in charge of the bordello, for he was shouting at the bouncers to silence them. The madam addressed him as Scanlon as she related what had happened.

Scanlon, a tall, blond man, looked nervously at Vince and Rosa. "What are you doin' with her down here?" he barked.

"I'm taking her with me," Vince replied. "We came here looking for her father, and she has no business in this place."

"You ain't takin' nobody nowhere!" Scanlon snarled. "Every woman in here has been bought and paid for, and they're stayin' right where they are. And you sure ain't gonna take that one out of here!"

"Why this one in particular?" Marshal Buell demanded, stepping forward.

The question created a momentary silence that Rosa broke in a thin, frightened voice: "Because I saw Big Jim Congor murder my father."

"What?" Buell exclaimed excitedly. "Rosa, are you sure of that?"

"I saw it with my own eyes! He stabbed my father, right in the saloon!" She let out a long sob and leaned against Vince.

"I'm mighty sorry to hear that, young lady," the marshal said softly. Then he turned to the captain. "Vince, let's get her out of here. I've finally found a witness against Congor, that piece of scum."

"She ain't goin' nowhere!" Scanlon bellowed, drawing his pistol with one hand and reaching for Rosa with the other.

The mob of people in the entry was suddenly a mass of confusion, with the madam squealing like a stuck pig and Rosa screaming as she tried to get behind Vince. Everyone else was shouting and shoving. The marshal drew his Colt, but by the time he had it out, Scanlon's gun was already leveled at him. Vince released Rosa to reach out and knock Scanlon's pistol away, but the motion only deflected it slightly.

The pistol fired with a deafening blast, filling the entry with gunpowder smoke. Shot through the right thigh, Marshal Buell went down with a bellow of rage and pain. Vince glanced down at him with concern and then looked up to see that Scanlon had Rosa's arm and was dragging her down the hall toward the rear of the building. Vince tried to race after the man but bumped into the madam, and the collision gave him the sensation of having run headlong into a foul-smelling mattress.

Disentangling himself from the heavy woman, Vince noticed that his father and Ira were wrestling with two of the bouncers. The third one, the huge man, was peering around, as though pondering what to do next, now that the marshal was down. After a long second, the need to go into action seemed to penetrate his dull brain, and the beady eyes under the beetling brows fastened on the captain. As Vince started for the rear of the hotel to rescue Rosa, the giant charged after him like a freight train, his massive arms open for a bear hug.

The huge man leapt for Vince's back but managed to grab only an arm. He stopped Vince and twirled him around, and the two men glared at each other for a few seconds. Then Vince lashed out, pounding with his fists and landing blows that were solid and well placed, but they had all the effect of raindrops. The huge man's hamlike arms closed around Vince, lifting him off the floor and pushing him back against the staircase rail. He felt the heavy rail sway and its supporting balusters break loose behind him as the man's arms tightened with a force that seemed to be crushing every bone in his chest and back.

Vince's knuckles stung as he slammed his fists against the man's head, but the arms continued tightening around him. The breath long since squeezed from his lungs, he felt unconsciousness approach. With all his strength, he spread his arms wide and then clapped his palms against the man's ears. The tactic worked, causing the bouncer to utter a shriek that sounded like a train whistle as he released Vince and clutched his head.

Vince sprawled among the loose balusters, wheezing and trying to catch his breath, while the bouncer stumbled across the entry and leaned against the wall in pain. Staggering to his feet, Vince picked up a baluster and stepped across the entry. He gathered himself and then whipped the thick length of wood down across the man's head.

Blood darkened the man's blond hair, but no other reaction to the blow was apparent. Taking a tighter grip on the baluster, Vince slashed it down on the man's head again. It was like hitting a brick wall, the shock of the impact traveling up Vince's arms and numbing them as the wood shattered into splinters. The bouncer, not even flinching, slowly turned his head and glared with bloodshot eyes. Then he charged again.

Backstepping rapidly, Vince stayed just out of reach of the bananalike fingers. The man lunged, grasping at Vince. Ducking aside, Vince put his shoulder against the broad back and added his own weight to the man's momentum, pushing him toward the staircase. The bouncer hit the staircase with a crash that sounded as if the building were collapsing as the remaining balusters crumbled and the rail broke apart.

Lying among the wreckage, the huge man was momentarily stunned. Vince picked up a section of the rail, a ten-foot length of solid oak that was four inches thick and six wide. The bouncer was starting to push himself to his hands and knees when Vince swept the rail down across his head and back. The staggering impact of the blow that shot through Vince's arms made him drop the rail, and the huge man fell flat once more.

The man immediately began stirring again, and Vince sighed wearily as he picked up the rail. Lifting it over his opponent's head, he rose to his tiptoes and then whipped the rail down. The thick wood split, and panting, Vince released the rail and flexed his fingers as he watched the bouncer warily for a second. Finally the man was unconscious.

Another bouncer had Harvey down on the floor, pounding him mercilessly. His arms still numbed, Vince stepped forward and kicked the man in the stomach with all his remaining strength, taking the bouncer by surprise. Clutching his stomach and retching, the man rolled off Harvey.

The third bouncer had Ira down and was choking him. Some of the feeling was starting to return to Vince's arm, and before the bouncer could rise up,

Vince took out his pistol and pounded the butt down on the man's head, knocking him away.

With all three of the bouncers down at last, Vince ran along the hall where Scanlon had taken Rosa. The alley door was standing open, and outside were fresh hoofprints where a horse had been tethered.

Running down the alley, Vince spotted a few loiterers and called to them, "Did a man and woman on horseback ride out of here a few minutes ago?"

One of the men nodded and then pointed toward the street and said, "They went that way."

Vince ran back to the entry, where Harvey and Ira, still breathless, were tying a temporary bandage on Buell's leg. "Scanlon took off on a horse with Rosa, and I'm going after him," Vince told them. "Dad, you and Ira take the marshal to see the doctor. I'll meet you there when I get back."

The three men nodded, and Vince ran out the door. Mounting up, he rode down the street in the direction the loiterers in the alley had indicated. The street led toward the southern edge of the town, and occasionally Vince shouted to bystanders to ask about a rider with a woman. Each one of them pointed down the street.

The street turned into the road that went past the Butler ranch, and Vince rode along it at a run. Seeing Elsie Butler in the pasture, he reined up and called to her, asking if she had seen a rider with a woman. She nodded and pointed toward a creek beside the road. Turning off the road, Vince found fresh hoofprints made by a horse that had been running.

The trail led straight west. As Vince was crossing a ridge a mile from town, he finally glimpsed Scanlon in the distance ahead, holding Rosa on his saddle and whipping his horse. In addition to carrying extra weight, the horse was weary, and the distance between Vince and Scanlon slowly closed.

When Vince was two hundred yards away, Scanlon looked back and saw him. The man took out his rifle and snapped off several shots, but the bullets harmlessly hit

the ground around Vince's horse. Vince took out his
rifle and held it as he leaned over his saddle. The man
was a moderately easy target, but the risk of hitting
Rosa was far too great. Closing the distance, he waited
for the right moment.

The magazine in Scanlon's rifle must have been
empty, since he gave up with that weapon and began to
fire his pistol. Vince saw that Rosa was offering no resistance. As she looked back at him, he could see that the
young woman was awaiting her chance to do what she
could to help. At a distance of a hundred yards, she
suddenly thrashed about and tried to throw herself
from the horse. Scanlon reined up and caught her as she
slid down the horse's side.

Vince pulled back on his reins and stopped his horse
as he lifted his rifle. Rosa was down beside the saddle,
giving him a clear shot at Scanlon. At the last instant,
Scanlon seemed to realize what had happened and
raised his pistol to fire, but the hammer on Vince's rifle
was already falling. The bullet punched through
Scanlon's heart as his pistol fired.

When her captor tumbled from his horse, Rosa also
fell from it and lay on the ground, sobbing. As Vince
rode forward and dismounted, she sprang up and ran to
him.

"Oh, Captain Bolton!" she cried, and as he took her in
his arms, she wept on his chest.

"It's all right, Rosa. It's all right. You're safe now.
You'll never have to go back there again."

After calming her, Vince walked her to his horse and
lifted her behind the saddle. Then he went back to
where Scanlon lay and hoisted his body across the saddle of his horse. Walking the outlaw's horse back to his
own, he mounted and rode back toward Socorro, leading the other horse.

In town people gaped at the body and followed as
Vince rode to the office of Dr. Harrison. Once there, he
helped Rosa down from the horse and took her inside.
Marshal Buell was sitting next to the physician's desk,

his right leg propped on a chair as Harrison attended to
his wound. No one had escaped unscathed, Vince
thought, feeling as though a wagon had run over him.
His father and Ira were there, too, both of them battered and bruised from their tussle with the bouncers.

Vince explained what had happened with Scanlon
and then pointed to Rosa. "You have your witness
against Congor now, Marshal."

The marshal winced as the doctor pulled the bandage
tight, then sighed and shook his head. "I'm not so sure
now, Vince. When Congor gets back, I'll collar him and
see what he has to say. But my guess is that he'll come
up with better witnesses to counter her testimony."

The lawman's meaning was clear: A woman from a
bordello was not a choice witness to put before a jury,
and Congor could probably devise some sort of alibi.
"Well, we'll see what happens," Harvey Bolton mused.
"In the meantime, we'll keep Rosa at the way station.
Nobody will bother her there, and Pilar can come to see
her. Will the marshal's leg be all right, Doctor Harrison?"

The aged, bearded doctor nodded confidently, knot-
ting the bandage. "The bullet went straight through
and left a clean wound. The marshal spends most of his
time on his backside anyway, so this shouldn't interfere
with his usual business to any great extent."

"Is that so?" Buell grumbled. "If it was you sitting
here hurting, you wouldn't be so all-fired cheerful about
it."

Vince laughed, and then taking Rosa's arm, he left
with her and his father. His smile faded as he thought
about what had happened. While he had resolved the
question about Antonio Montero and had rescued Rosa
from the bordello, those accomplishments were
blighted by the tragedy and the torment that the young
woman had endured.

More than ever, Vince longed for a way to make
Congor pay for his crimes and to rid the town of the
man.

Chapter Five

Two days after setting out, Big Jim Congor arrived in Santa Fe at midday after a hard ride, during which he had exhausted four horses. At first it appeared to him that he had wasted his time, money, and effort in making the journey. As he went from one saloon to another, virtually all of the men he talked to had heard about the Spaniards who had been in Santa Fe, and some had even seen them, but no one knew anything of importance about them. They had kept very much to themselves.

Congor had learned one thing that might prove helpful—the location of the house the Spaniards had stayed in. Driving there in his buggy, he guided his horse through the wide carriage gate at the edge of the street. As he pulled into the courtyard, he saw a man cutting weeds in the garden at the side of the house.

The workman, a grubby, unshaven man with a sullen expression, stepped around the house and said, "What do you want, mister?"

Congor smiled amiably. "I need to rent a house, and I heard this one is available."

"You'll have to see the owner," the man said with a surly shrug. "I just work for him, doin' chores around the grounds."

"Have you worked for him very long?"

"A few months," the man replied warily. "Why do you wanna know?"

"Just making conversation, my friend," Congor said, concealing his satisfaction. "You know, I feel like having a drink, but I hate to drink alone. Do you have time to join me?"

The workman blinked, taken aback by the invitation, and then his expression changed, as if the idea of a free drink was too tempting to turn down, even from a stranger. As he climbed into the buggy, he introduced himself as Elmer Keenan. Congor turned toward the gate and drove back through the streets, stopping at the first saloon he came to. He and Keenan went inside and took seats at a table near the bar.

Finding Keenan at first reluctant to talk about the Spaniards, Congor did not press the subject. The man's unwillingness to talk about the Carranzas seemed promising to Congor, suggesting that the man knew something he intended to turn to personal advantage. He was a type of man that Congor knew well, having hired many of them.

Once the whiskey began loosening his tongue, the workman became less cautious about what he said and revealed that he knew much about the Spaniards. After a sarcastic comment about pampered wealthy people, he named the servants they had with them and talked about the young woman's beauty, his voice heavy with lust.

After making a few more remarks about the Carranzas, Keenan ventured onto other topics. He revealed that he had had scrapes with the law in various places and had spent time in jail. He also mentioned a friend he had in El Paso, who had recently served a term in Arizona's territorial prison for a stagecoach holdup. "I should be hearing from him pretty soon," he mused. "I wrote him last week, and he should have the let—" He broke off with an expression of having said too much. After knocking down the rest of the whiskey in his glass, he said, "So you're movin' to Santa Fe, are you?"

"Yes, in the very near future," Congor replied.

Well on his way to being drunk, Keenan frowned suspiciously. "Why are you buyin' me so many drinks?"

"Because I enjoy your company, of course."

The answer seemed to satisfy the man. Congor went to the bar, bought another bottle, and they continued to drink.

Another casual remark from Congor about the Carranzas started Keenan on the right track again. "I heard the servants talkin' among themselves, and I found out somethin' very few people know," he said, his voice slurred. "I understood enough of what they said to figure out why they're here."

"It has to do with a dead priest, doesn't it?" Congor ventured.

"That's right, a priest from their family who died durin' the Indian uprisin' two hundred years ago. They wanna get his bones and plant 'em in a churchyard, so they must know where the bones are. And what's with those bones will make me rich. See, my friend can get plenty of men and guns to ambush 'em—" He broke off, looking at Congor in confusion, and then began to stand. "I have to go home," he mumbled. "I'm drunk."

Congor walked with the man to the buggy and took him as far as the Carranzas' drive. As soon as they had stopped, he took out his derringer and pulled back the hammers, pointing the tiny pistol at the inebriated man's head. "Where are they going, Keenan?"

Looking into the pistol barrels seemed to sober the man. His face became taut, his eyes glassy with fear. He hesitated, licking his lips dryly, and then spoke softly. "Gran Quivira," he whispered.

Everything was suddenly clear to Congor. The stories he had heard about the fabulous lost treasure of Gran Quivira raced through his mind. Lost during the Pueblo revolt, the treasure had most likely been taken by the priest when he fled. Now the Carranzas had come from Spain for their relative's remains, knowing where they were. The treasure would be there, also.

Keenan lifted a hand and screamed as Congor fired

the pistol. The first bullet went through the workman's palm, knocking his hand aside and punching a hole in his forehead. Congor leaned over and put the second bullet in the back of the man's head; then he dumped the limp form from the buggy.

Driving south from Santa Fe, Congor mentally revised his plan to take advantage of the priceless information he had obtained. The valuables at the Gran Quivira mission were reputed to have included large, solid-gold crosses, gold altar vessels encrusted with precious stones, and other riches. What he had learned opened up an opportunity for vast wealth.

It was the chance of a lifetime, and the only one who knew that he had the secret information was now dead. Congor could almost feel the sensually smooth, heavy gold in his hands. In other undertakings he had made plans and parceled out tasks among his men, but this job he would plan on his own. He was unwilling to trust his men with so much wealth, and he wanted to seize the gold personally and bring it back to Socorro.

He also wanted personally to kill Vince Bolton. In the arid wastelands between Socorro and Gran Quivira, Bolton and all those with him could be annihilated, and the authorities would never know who did it. It would remain a mystery, since their location was supposed to be a secret.

But his mission involved risks. A cavalry escort accompanied Bolton and the Spaniards, and Indians roamed the region surrounding Gran Quivira. Even so, Congor was confident of being able to assemble enough men to overcome the escort, and he could avoid the Indians by remaining in the eastern foothills of the Los Piños Mountains. There he could ambush the party on their return trip, when they would be weary and their animals would probably be lame—and when they would have the gold.

Returning to Socorro late in the evening, Big John Congor was met by the news of what had happened at the hotel. Slumped in a chair in his sitting room, he puffed on a cigar and sipped a glass of whiskey as he listened to Frable relate the events, the man's face swollen and bruised from Vince Bolton's knuckles. Seething with frustrated rage, Congor knew that he had to resist giving in to his anger, and he carefully weighed what he had to do.

The next morning, freshly shaven and wearing a clean suit in a bright red and yellow check, Congor went in his buggy to the marshal's office. Buell, sitting behind his desk with one foot propped on a chair, looked up with an angry frown. "So you're back in town, Congor," he said. "If I'd known that, I would have sent a deputy to arrest you."

"Arrest me?" Congor echoed in bland surprise. "Whatever for, Marshal Buell? I heard you had been shot, so I came to see how you're doing."

"Yes, I was shot," Buell growled. "And by one of your men, Congor."

"While you, your deputy, and the Boltons were wrecking my hotel," Congor pointed out smoothly. "Nevertheless, I was going to bring the man and turn him in, but I found out that Bolton killed him. I'm not one to hold grudges, though, and I hope you heal up soon."

"I don't need your good wishes, Congor!" Buell snapped. "I have an eyewitness who saw you murder Antonio Montero."

"Is that right?" Congor chuckled. "Well, I have a dozen witnesses who will testify that Montero decided to leave town, and that I gave him a bonus and my best wishes before he left."

Buell ground his teeth in rage, pointing a finger. "Sooner or later, I'll get something on you that'll stick, Congor."

"No, you won't, Marshal Buell," Congor assured him, turning to the door. "You see, I'm simply a businessman and a law-abiding citizen, and I have nothing to fear. Good day to you, Marshal."

A continuing undercurrent of anger toward Bolton marring his otherwise good mood, Congor returned to the Sundowner and summoned Lew Frable to his rooms. Frable, still unaware of where Congor had been or the purpose of his trip, asked how it went.

"It's none of your business, Frable," Congor snapped, dismissing the subject. "Have you found out any more about Bolton and those Spaniards?"

"Nothin' to amount to anythin', Big Jim. Jake Clinton told me that there are twenty cavalrymen with them, but everybody in town knows that. Bolton has supplies of all kinds packed on those wagons, but nobody has any idea about where he's takin' those Spaniards. They're leaving soon, I heard."

Pondering the possibility that Jake Clinton might mention all the free drinks Frable had plied him with to Harvey Bolton, Congor decided to put a halt to the questioning. "Clinton has done us all the good he will, so end his free drinks." Then, puffing on his cigar, he asked, "If we needed plenty of help on a job, we could count on thirty men, couldn't we?"

"More than that, Big Jim."

"I know, but we'd need to leave several here." Congor thought for a moment and then said, "All right, the first thing I want you to do is spread the word that I intend to go look at some silver claims in the mountains west of here, and I'm taking men with me. People will notice thirty men taking off with me, and that'll satisfy curiosity. I want it spread all over town."

Frable flashed his yellow teeth in a grin. "That'll be easy to do, Big Jim."

"Then I want enough supplies to last thirty men for about a month, but I don't want to draw as much attention as Bolton has. For at least part of the time we'll have to eat food that doesn't need to be cooked."

"Sure thing. I'll make up some lists and buy the things at different places in small lots. When are we leavin'?"

Congor peered at him with disdain. "It'll be a few days."

"Everythin' will be taken care of, and it'll be done right. There's a whole bunch of men downstairs who've been waitin' to see you."

"Very well, I'll be down directly."

Frable left, and Congor finished his cigar and drink as he savored with anticipation the scheme he had hatched. The information about the treasure had awakened something deep within him, a raging hunger that had to be satisfied—even at the risk of his life.

Two days after Vince, his cavalrymen, and the Spaniards had pulled out of Socorro to begin their journey to Gran Quivira, Harvey Bolton was standing on the porch of the way station office, frowning as he watched Jake Clinton replacing a rail in the corral. The handyman had always been cheerful and needed little to make him happy, but for days now he had been quiet. Something was obviously bothering him. Harvey had asked him several times if anything was wrong, but Clinton had denied it. Now, his bad leg twinging, Harvey stepped off the porch and crossed his compound toward the corral to question the man again.

"Jake, we've been together a few years now," he said, "and I'd like to think that we can talk man to man with each other."

"Why, we can, Mr. Bolton," Clinton replied, stepping away from the fence and surveying his work. "Am I doing something wrong here?"

"No, no, you're doing a good job, Jake. What I'm thinking about is the way you've been acting. I'm sure something is bothering you."

The man shook his head stubbornly and went back to hammering at the rail. "No, there's nothing wrong, Mr. Bolton."

"Well, I think there is, and you're keeping it to yourself, Jake. I've told you many times before that I'm more than glad to help you with any problems, even if they're personal."

The handyman, pounding furiously at the rail, simply nodded.

Harvey sighed and shrugged, knowing he could do nothing more. He turned away to walk back to the office, but then the hammering suddenly stopped.

"I betrayed Vince!" Clinton blurted in distress.

Harvey turned back. Clinton's face was red, and the man was almost in tears with shame. "What do you mean, Jake?" Harvey asked.

"You know that man Frable, who works for Congor? Well, he asked me a bunch of questions about Mr. Vince and the Spaniards, and I told him all I knew about them, Mr. Bolton."

Apprehensive that Clinton might somehow have overheard the destination, Harvey frowned. "Did you tell Frable where they're going, Jake?"

"Why, no, Mr. Bolton. Mr. Vince and the Spaniards are the only ones who know that, aren't they?"

"It should be kept a secret, Jake," Harvey answered. "What did you tell Frable, then?"

The handyman related his conversation with Frable, and Harvey was relieved that almost everything was more or less commonly known throughout Socorro. When Clinton was done, Harvey said, "I've warned you not to have anything to do with people like Frable, Jake, but no harm was done. Just forget it happened, because it isn't worth worrying about."

"I'm sure glad of that!" Clinton exclaimed happily. "I wouldn't have had anything to do with him, but he bought me a lot of drinks."

Harvey pursed his lips reflectively. "He did?"

Clinton nodded. Turning back to his work, the handyman hummed cheerfully as he hammered on the rail.

Harvey returned to the office and sat down at his desk, pondering what Clinton had told him. He was worried that Frable—and hence Congor—had been interested in Vince and the Spaniards. Congor was an expert at exploiting people, and he had ample reason to want something on Vince he could use. Undoubtedly that had been Frable's purpose, but judging from what Jake Clinton had just said, Frable had been unable to give Congor any new information. Nevertheless Harvey felt uneasy. He decided to ride into Socorro and discuss the issue with the marshal.

Harvey found Alfred Buell in his office with Ira Chapman and related what Jake had told him. The marshal, his right leg heavily bandaged, sat silently for a moment. Then he said, "This doesn't sound good, Harv. Congor and most of his men have left town. They're reportedly off looking at silver claims west of here, but if he knows about Don Raimundo's mission, it's possible he's following Vince."

"Well, what do you think we should do, Fred?" Harvey asked, worried about his son. "Should we contact that Colonel Hamilton in Santa Fe and get him to send somebody to warn Vince?"

"No, that would take too long. Congor could be on the road to Gran Quivira right now." Looking at his deputy, Buell said, "Whoever goes to warn Vince will have to skirt through the mountains, all the while keeping himself invisible from Congor and his men—if they *are* after Vince. That's a job for a young man, not one who's getting on in years. Do you feel up to a little trip, Ira?"

"I'll be glad to go, Marshal," Ira Chapman said, rising. "But you'll have to tell me where Vince and the others are headed."

Harvey explained the destination and the purpose of the trip. When he had finished, Ira said, "It'll be best if I leave right away. I can go pick up my tack, buy a few supplies, and still have time to make it close to the foothills by dark. That'll put me in a good position to find a route around the road first thing tomorrow morning."

"Yes, that would be best, Ira," Buell agreed.

Harvey took a sheet of paper and a pencil from the desk and wrote a brief message to his son, explaining what he had found out and the potential danger. After folding it and giving it to Ira, he took out his wallet. "Ira, the least I can do is pay for your supplies." Taking money from his wallet, he handed it to the man. "There, and I want you to know that I certainly appreciate what you're doing."

The young deputy shrugged off Harvey's thanks. Shaking hands with him and the marshal, he left. As he went off, Harvey shook his head and said to the marshal, "I don't know, Fred. I just don't feel too comfortable with this. Ira's putting himself in a lot of danger."

"Ira will watch out for himself. He's plenty smart," the marshal answered.

"Yes," Harvey observed quietly, "but so is Congor."

Chapter Six

As early morning sunlight beamed down on the western foothills of the Los Piños Mountains, Lew Frable sat at the edge of a clearing and watched the road that led up to the hills. Big Jim Congor had instructed him to take three men and travel a good distance behind the others, just in case anyone was following them. Congor was worried that someone from Socorro would figure out that he and his men were not looking at silver claims west of town but were instead trailing Vince Bolton and the Spaniards to the east. Frable's job was to see that such a messenger never reached the captain and his party.

While Frable knew that Congor had no intention of looking at silver claims, he had no idea why his boss, the other men, and he were following Bolton and his party at a distance of several miles and going without campfires to avoid detection. Although he was Congor's second-in-command, Frable reflected, he rarely knew more about his employer's plans than any of the other men. At the same time, he was content merely to follow orders. He was well paid, had authority over the other men, and no longer had to fear the tap on the shoulder by a policeman that would result in a jail sentence for picking pockets.

As his three men moved about in the trees behind Frable, washing down their cold rations with gulps of water and rolling up their blankets, they were silent.

Leaning back against trees, they gazed to the west,
looking in the same direction as Frable. The minutes
passed, turning into an hour. As the sun moved higher,
the shadows cast by the trees at the edge of the clearing
became thinner. Frable was just on the point of telling
the men to move back into the deeper shadows between the trees when one of them pointed.

Training his binoculars on the rider in the distance,
Frable examined him. The man was well to the south of
the road but riding almost parallel to it, and he disappeared into some trees a moment after Frable saw him.
Scanning the terrain ahead of the rider, Frable waited.
Presently, the man came into view again as he crossed
an opening in the trees, but he was too far away for
Frable to make out his features. A few minutes later, the
rider emerged from the trees into open woods on the
shoulder of a hill.

Gradually the man drew closer, traveling in a line
that would take him south of Frable and his men. Straining his eyes as he peered through the binoculars, Frable
recognized him, a part-time deputy in Socorro named
Chapman, and he smiled with satisfaction. A stranger
would have left some doubt in his mind about whether
he was looking for Vince or was riding this way for
another purpose, but Frable knew that Chapman was a
likely choice for carrying a message to Bolton.

"All right, that's the man we've been watchin' for,"
Frable said, lowering the binoculars and turning toward
the horses. "And this is as far as he's gonna get. Follow
me and keep quiet."

He led the men to a long, wide ravine that stretched
away to the south. When they were several hundred
yards from where they had been watching the road,
Frable reined up. He and the men dismounted, and
after they had tethered the horses, he quietly led them
to the top of the ridge on the west side of the ravine.

Ira Chapman rode slowly up the slope below, picking
his way through trees and boulders. Frable cocked his
rifle and aimed it, tracking Chapman with the sights.

He squeezed the trigger, and the other men also fired. Chapman reeled in the saddle as he wheeled his horse around. Cursing under his breath, Frable worked the lever on his rifle and fired again as Chapman leaned over the saddle and began riding away. Then the man fell from his horse.

"We got him, Frable!" one of the men yelped.

"Shut up and get after that horse! I don't want it to wander back into Socorro. Get your horses and catch it," Frable snapped. Pointing to one of the men, he added, "You, come with me."

The two men ran for their horses, and the third followed Frable as he made his way down the slope. As he approached the place where Ira Chapman had been when the firing began, Frable peered ahead cautiously, knowing that the man was probably only wounded. He spotted the deputy's legs on the other side of a boulder, and stepping around it, he snatched Chapman's pistol away as the deputy weakly reached for it. Shot through the chest and stomach, Chapman tried to resist as Frable searched him, but the struggling ended when Frable clubbed the man with the butt of his rifle.

Looking through Chapman's pockets, Frable found the message and read:

> Vince,
>   There's a good chance that Congor and his men are following you. Keep an eye out—and be careful.
>
>   Dad

Glowing with satisfaction, Frable folded the paper and stuck it in his pocket. "This is just what we've been waitin' for," he said happily. "Now we can catch up with Big Jim and the rest of 'em."

"We don't have to worry about him," the man with Frable remarked, pointing to Chapman. "He won't last long."

"No, he surely won't." Frable chuckled grimly, taking out his knife. "Hold him down."

The man gripped Chapman's arms and held them as the deputy struggled feebly, his eyes glassy with pain and rage. Frable leaned over and slit his throat; then he wiped the knife on the deputy's shirt. After putting the knife away, he glanced up at the sun. "Go get the horses. I wanna catch up with Big Jim and the others today, and we've got some ground to cover."

The man hurried back up the slope and then returned a few minutes later with the horses from the ravine. The other two rode up, leading the deputy's horse. Frable looked it over, making sure it had not been wounded by the gunfire, and told the men to bring it along. Then he mounted his horse and led them toward the road.

Frable whipped his horse to a rapid pace, its hooves kicking up bits of weed and brush. He was eager to reach Congor and please him with the good news. Only when his horse began panting breathlessly and stumbling did he grudgingly slow down, and then for just a short period of time, hardly long enough for the animal to rest.

At midday the men complained that they wanted to stop to rest and eat. But glaring back at them, Frable bellowed for silence, and they went on.

The hours of the afternoon dragged by, and Frable pushed on, eager to tell Congor of his success. It was nearing evening when he rounded a curve and saw the other men ahead, picketing the horses and making camp beside a stream.

Congor, who disliked traveling by horseback, was sitting at one side of the camp, an ill-tempered expression on his wattled face. He was clearly out of his element in the wilderness, and his rumpled, gaudy suit made him appear all the more ineffectual. He took a swig from his whiskey flask and glowered at Frable irately. "You'd better have good reason for being here," he snarled. "I gave you a job to do, and I expect it to be done right."

"It has been, Big Jim," Frable assured him anxiously, taking out the message. "Here, look at this. That's one problem we can forget about."

As Congor read the message, his frown faded, and then he laughed gleefully. "This is what I was worried about, all right," he said, tearing the message into bits. "Who was carrying it?"

"That man named Chapman who works for Buell as a deputy."

"Well, well. About the only thing that would make me happier is if it had been that old gimp who runs the way station in Socorro. But I'll get him sooner or later. Frable, you did a good job."

The weasel-faced man sat down, preening in Congor's approval. "I always do my best for you, Big Jim, you know that. One thing worries me, though. From that message I'd say they know we're here, so they'll know who took care of Chapman when everythin' settles down, once this whole business is over. Killin' a lawman can cause trouble."

"They might know who took care of him, but proving it is something else. All I worry about is what people can prove, not what they think."

Frable grinned and nodded, relieved that Congor did not feel that their having killed a deputy was a threat. Glancing around at the men sullenly going about the chores of making camp, Frable stated, "You know, Big Jim, the men would be a lot happier if they could build fires. It gets fearfully cold at night."

"They'll be able to build fires a few days after we reach the other side of the mountains," Congor said. "They may as well be happy for a while, because we're riding in here with a lot more men than we'll be riding out with. That's the way I planned it, because when people look into what happened, nobody can blame me for what a bunch of men decide to do. In the meantime, the men will do as they're told."

"They sure will," Frable agreed quickly, "because everybody knows you're the boss, Big Jim." Having learned that Bolton and his party were to be ambushed, as he had expected, Frable probed indirectly to find out more. "You know, at the rate we've been travelin', we could've left Socorro a week later and still been here in plenty of time."

"Getting here in time wasn't the only thing involved," Congor growled. "I wanted to make certain I had Bolton bottled up so he couldn't get away. You just follow orders and leave everything else to me, Frable."

Hastily assuring Congor that he was content to follow orders, Frable dropped the subject. He knew that Congor's overpowering hatred of Captain Vince Bolton would make him go to great lengths to kill the man, but more than that had to be involved. There was an underlying reason behind this trip, and it remained a mystery to him.

A brisk breeze stirred the wind-gnarled brush around the Mescalero warrior named Dark Cloud as he lay on a high ridge and studied the scene below. Far down the cascade of forested slopes he watched a column made up of four wagons, a stagecoach, and many riders—mostly soldiers—moving slowly up the narrow road that wound its tortuous way into the mountains. With only a few settlers widely scattered in the foothills of the mountains, and most of them far to the north, the road was rarely used. Certainly no group of travelers even approaching the size of the column had ever used it.

Dark Cloud found it strange and perplexing that such a party would travel this route, but he was indifferent about their reason for being there. For him it was a long-awaited opportunity that had finally presented itself. His eyes riveted to the caravan on the road below, he seethed with fierce excitement.

A Mescalero half-breed in his late twenties, Dark Cloud had always been acutely conscious of being different from those around him. At an early age he had noticed his physical differences, his green eyes, his light-brown hair, and his pale skin. He had also been keenly aware that his father had never returned to the reservation, as his mother promised he would.

Rebellious from early boyhood, he had been the source of many conflicts, which had grown more serious as he became older. Two years before, he had joined the Mescalero Apache chief White Eagle, who could not conform to life on the reservation. The chief chose to live instead as his ancestors had, roaming free in the wilderness, and Dark Cloud had followed him, but not from respect; the young warrior was loyal to no one and respected no authority. Dark Cloud's only motivation in joining White Eagle's band was his secret ambition to gain prestige and eventually replace White Eagle as chief. Since the chief controlled the warriors, whom Dark Cloud needed to prove himself to the other Mescaleros, he feigned subservience and loyalty.

After a year of persistent effort, Dark Cloud had convinced White Eagle to designate him a leading warrior and place him in charge of a foraging party. Since then he had performed better than any other leading warrior, returning to the main encampment in Mexico with ample game and stolen animals. During each of those forays, however, Dark Cloud had searched for an opportunity to prove himself as a war leader. With a dramatic victory to boast about, young warriors would join him of their own accord, and his position as a leading warrior would be impregnable.

Once Dark Cloud had assumed White Eagle's place as chief, he intended to replace the chief's methods with his own, spreading a reign of terror over the region. That would draw more warriors off the reservation to join him, and the name of Dark Cloud would become as well known as that of Geronimo.

But finding the chance to show his strength was proving to be a difficult task for Dark Cloud—because of White Eagle's restrictions. The chief had given strict orders to all leading warriors that animals were to be stolen from farms and ranches only through stealth, not by attacks. He had warned that harming settlers would bring retaliation down upon all of his followers. He had even more emphatically ordered that any risk of battle with cavalry was to be avoided.

Many warriors, particularly the younger ones, grumbled about the timid measures that White Eagle enforced. They obeyed him, however, out of loyalty and respect for his authority. Dark Cloud had also obeyed the chief's orders, but only to keep from being removed as a leading warrior.

Now, as he watched the long column of soldiers on horseback, the wagons, and the coach, Dark Cloud began to think that his waiting was over. The chance to prove himself in battle was close at hand.

The day before, far behind the column, he had spotted a second group, all on horseback, who seemed to be following the column. Since then he had been watching the progress of the two groups and had concluded that the second group was following the first with evil intent. Why else would they not want to be seen? They had been moving up the road at the same pace as the column far ahead, even though they were unburdened with wagons and capable of traveling much faster. They had no campfires, apparently to avoid being detected by those they were following.

The travelers in the column were much more disciplined and organized than the riders following them. The wagons maintained even intervals except when they stopped, and the soldiers were always deployed around the wagons and coach in defensive positions, ready to protect them on every side with a hail of bullets. The leader of the soldiers chose campsites that took full advantage of the natural cover in the mountains, places that were easy to defend. That, combined with the sentries that were always posted, would make a night attack perilous, but Dark Cloud would chance it if doing so would gain him a victory.

The travelers apparently intended to go across the mountains to the flatlands on the other side. One option, Dark Cloud decided, was to wait until the column reached the flatlands, where there was little natural cover. There, a night attack would be less dangerous and the chances of being able to steal the horses would be far better. A second option was to capture the soldiers who rode ahead during the late afternoon to scout for a campsite, or the woman who rode with the leader at the front of the column. Occasionally she ventured ahead or off to one side, leaving her vulnerable.

The brush and weeds rustled, and Dark Cloud looked up to see one of his twelve warriors creeping up beside him. The warrior looked down at the column and then turned to his leader. "Why do you watch them?" the warrior asked. "Are we not to hunt game to take back to the main camp?"

"Return to the others!" Dark Cloud ordered curtly. "You will be told all you need to know in good time."

Dark Cloud pondered his situation as the warrior left. His men needed to be told something to make them assist him in his act of aggression against the travelers, yet he knew they would not consent to going against White Eagle's orders.

Quietly, Dark Cloud left his position to rejoin the warriors, who had been working busily. One was fleshing out the deerskins from the buck they had killed earlier in the day, while the others were roasting and drying strips of venison over beds of hot coals. The sliced livers from the deer were cooking over another fire, and the warriors were munching pieces of it as they worked.

Once he had been at the camp for a while, it was obvious to Dark Cloud that the warriors were perplexed and apprehensive about his interest in the travelers and were wondering why they were not hunting for food to take back to the main encampment. As he sat beside the tiny campfire and ate a strip of venison, he revealed his plan to them, though the version he told involved a degree of deception.

"As you know, I have been closely watching the travelers. The group in the lead has many horses, far more

than the second group, which follows far enough behind not to interfere. The travelers are careless with
their animals, and at night the horses are not hobbled
correctly. Some have even strayed. Warriors, our people have need of horses! Horses are scarce! We will take
the horses that the white travelers do not care for!"

The warriors became excited, eager to get the young,
strong horses that Dark Cloud described. He explained
that they could go close to the road and look for straying
horses, but they had to be extremely cautious not to
violate White Eagle's orders to avoid battle with
soldiers.

In a chorus of excited voices, the warriors assured
Dark Cloud that they would be cautious if he would
lead them to the horses the next day.

Dark Cloud smirked with pleasure at the ease with
which his men had been convinced to follow him. Unknown to them, he had decided to take a hostage. If that
failed, he would wait until the travelers reached the
flatlands east of the mountains and plan a night attack.

Chapter Seven

On the third day of the journey, at a narrow curve in the road, with a sheer drop of a hundred feet on one side and a steep rock face on the other, Captain Vince Bolton saw five of his soldiers ahead, standing in a group. Riding closer, he realized that they were straining at a thick tree limb, which they were using as a lever to move a boulder that had fallen on the road, blocking it. He dismounted and called for two more soldiers to join him. "Come on, let's give them a hand, troopers," he ordered.

The five men at the limb relaxed, panting. Vince found a place among them to put his shoulder to the limb, and the other two joined him. "Now all together, troopers," he said. "Push!"

The limb creaked as the men threw their weight against it. The boulder moved slowly and then toppled, rolling off the edge of the road and crashing through trees, starting a rockslide below. Heaving a sigh of relief, the soldiers tossed the limb over the edge and returned to their horses.

Vince stepped into his saddle and then walked his horse to where the boulder had been. He looked at the stagecoach on the other side of the curve and called to the driver, "Are you sure you can get the coach around now, Culley?"

"Yes, Captain Bolton. It'll be easy now," the man replied, and then he shook the reins and whistled to the horses.

Harness chains rattled as the stagecoach rumbled forward. Vince knew that Don Raimundo was safely inside, poring over a book, as he did for hours each day. When the captain saw that the coach had many inches to spare on the curve, he glanced around for Arabella. She had been with Murillo and the soldiers at the head of the column only moments before. Now she was gone, although he had warned her repeatedly not to wander off.

"Where is Señorita Arabella?" he called to Murillo, who was standing nearest to him.

Murillo, his swarthy features set in their usual sullen expression, shrugged indifferently and pointed up the road.

Biting back a sharp remark, Vince reined his horse around, and a stab of anxiety rushed through him. His horse sprang into a canter, quickly covering the short distance to the next curve in the narrow, twisting road. When he saw Arabella ahead, Vince sighed with relief.

Mounted on her horse, she was looking at a brilliant display of yellow mariposa lilies that covered a glade in the woods beside the road. She turned to Vince with a smile as he rode up. "Are they not lovely, Vincent?" she exclaimed. "You have such lovely flowers here. It is more than worth the journey just to see them."

"I've told you to stay with the column, Arabella!" Vince said sternly. "This was a very senseless thing for you to do!"

Upon hearing his harsh tone, the delight on her face turned to surprise.

Vince mentally castigated himself for raising his voice. He should have been more insistent when he cautioned her to stay with the column, rather than exploding in anger now. While she was headstrong and accustomed to doing as she wished, Arabella was also warm and caring, and certainly not spoiled. The shock

on her beautiful face tormented him, and he bit back
the angry words he had in mind.

What he really wanted to do was enfold Arabella in
his arms and hold her tight. The flowers were indeed
lovely, but they were merely a pleasant backdrop when
compared to this strikingly beautiful young woman. He
found that he was charmed even by her willful nature,
although it was proving to be a problem for him on the
journey.

"Yes, the flowers are pretty," he agreed. "But, Arabella, you mustn't venture off by yourself."

"Very well," she replied. She was silent for a few
moments, as though the sting of his rebuke was still
troubling her. But in a moment, she looked up at him
shyly and said, "Vincent, I would like to gather the
seeds of all these flowers we are seeing."

He smiled at her childlike tone. "They aren't in seed
yet, and they won't be for several months. Arabella, I'm
sorry that I snapped at you. But please, do stay near the
soldiers at all times."

Sighing with resignation, she nodded and lifted her
reins as the soldiers came around the curve, the stagecoach and the wagons following them. Vince rode the
distance with her at a walk, looking back to make certain the vehicles and soldiers flanking them had resumed their correct positions after the short delay.

His glance passed over Murillo, who was seated on his
horse. The small man's face was pinched in its persistent scowl, and turning back to Arabella, Vince asked,
"What can you tell me about Murillo?"

Her dark eyes flashing with mischief, she gave him a
sly smile. "He is a sour man, is he not? He probably
dislikes being here, Vincent. It is most likely an inconvenience to his work in the foreign ministry. Also, he
belongs to a political faction that is a rival of my father's
party."

Finding this odd, Vince asked, "Then why is he working for the government?"

"Exiling rival factions from the government merely

gives them the perfect opportunity to plot in secret—
and plenty of time to create discontent among our citizens. Incorporating rivals into the government dilutes
their influence and demonstrates open-mindedness to
the public. In addition, many of them are talented, use-
ful people."

Vince laughed and shook his head as his horse continued forward. "I could never be a politician."

"Many people could not, Vincent. But many could
not be an exemplary soldier, as you are."

He smiled warmly at Arabella. As they rode on in
silence, he realized that this journey was turning into
the happiest time of his life. There had been moments
of anxiety, of course, such as when Arabella had wan-
dered off; yet at the same time, having to keep track of
her constantly was in itself gratifying. Articulate and
well informed, she was a fascinating companion. However, his pleasure was shadowed by the certainty that in
time she would return to Spain . . . and to the Duke of
Valencia.

Dark Cloud seethed with frustrated rage. When the
black-haired woman had left the others in her party, he
and the warriors had been in a good position to inter-
cept her. He had been preparing to spring out at her
when the leader of the soldiers rushed up on his horse.

Knowing he would have succeeded if he had acted
quickly, Dark Cloud ground his teeth in fury, regretting
his moments of hesitation. Then he forced aside his
anger over the failed opportunity and thought about
what he should do next. Continuing to shadow the column in the mountains had little promise, and the muttering among the warriors indicated they would object
strongly. That left an attack at night on the column
when it reached the flatlands.

At the horses, the muttering among the warriors became louder and more direct. One of them commented
that he had seen no horses straying from the column,

and another said that the spare horses had been tethered.

"They are being more careful with their horses now,"
Dark Cloud said, shrugging. "If we had acted sooner,
we could have had extra horses now."

"We were not going to get horses," another warrior
remarked cautiously. "You wanted to capture the
woman. That would have been against White Eagle's
orders, Dark Cloud."

"I have discussed White Eagle's orders with him
many times," Dark Cloud lied blandly. "He agrees with
me that there are times when a leading warrior must
use his judgment. We do not attack farms and ranches,
but what do we do when they attack us? Do we fight, or
do Mescalero warriors run from a battle like rabbits?"

The warriors frowned as they emphatically replied
that they must fight. "We do not risk a battle with
soldiers," Dark Cloud continued. "If I had captured the
woman, there would have been no risk of battle. There
would only have been many horses traded to get her
back. But when the soldier arrived, there was a risk of
battle, so we remained hidden."

"Perhaps we can capture her later," a warrior suggested.

"No, we will not be able to. When she and the leader
spoke, they used the language of Mexico, which White
Eagle and I speak well. She will not leave the others
again."

"What will we do now, Dark Cloud?" a warrior asked.

"Hunt for food," he replied, turning to his horse.
"Come."

As he mounted his horse and led the warriors back
toward the higher elevations, Dark Cloud pondered his
plans. For the rest of the day he would keep the warriors in the mountains, hunting deer. Then he would
lead them to an isolated ranch he had seen in the eastern foothills, adjacent to the road.

He would tell the warriors they were there to steal
livestock; then he would lead them so the rancher

would be certain to see them, bringing gunfire. The warriors would retaliate, killing everyone at the ranch.

A warrior or two would be wounded or killed, he mused, but the foraging party would still be strong enough for a night attack on the column when it was in the flatlands. And after taking a few scalps at the ranch, the warriors would be in the right mood for the attack.

The narrow road was overgrown with weeds and brush that appeared to have been undisturbed for years. Following the path of least resistance, it wound around contours in the mountains and led from one valley to another, slowly climbing toward a pass at the crest of the range. It presented an ever-changing scene of pristine wilderness beauty, the dense growths of fir and aspen on the mountains above alternating with meadows bright with wildflowers and rock faces that caught the afternoon sun in a brilliant range of hues.

From Vince's point of view, however, the road abounded with hazards. He was unable to see ahead or behind the twists in the road, and only the slopes above were in open view. Each curve and overhanging bluff was a good position for an ambush, and he had the soldiers deployed so they could defend against attack from any direction.

A movement in a meadow above caught his eye, and Vince looked up to see a deer race across an opening in the trees almost a mile away. Turning in his saddle, he glanced back and saw that Sergeant Henshaw had also noticed the deer. The sergeant spurred his horse forward. "That was much closer than before, Captain Bolton," he said.

Nodding, Vince studied the meadow. At various times during the past day, he and the sergeant had observed disturbances among the wildlife, but the movements had been higher up in the mountains. "Yes, and the deer was running downhill. Whatever frightened it was doing the same. One possible explanation is that Indians are watching the column." He turned to

Henshaw. "Close up the intervals between the stage-coach and wagons to ten feet. Take two troopers away from the rear guard and add them to the flanks. Order the troop to lock and load."

The sergeant saluted, and spurring his horse, he wheeled it around. "Troop!" he bellowed. "Lock and load!"

As the soldiers took out their carbines and loaded rounds into the firing chambers in a metallic clatter of bolts opening and closing, Vince turned to Arabella to reassure her. "Having the men load their weapons to fire is mostly a means of making them more alert," he said. "I've seen nothing to indicate we're in any immediate danger."

Arabella smiled at Vince, and he was relieved that she did not seem to be hurt by his earlier rebuke.

The column followed the road as it dipped into a valley. A wide stream babbled over rocks beside the road as it curved along the valley to the far end. Off to one side at the head of the valley, rocks and trees were arranged around an opening in a way that made three sides of it a natural fortress, the kind of place Vince always chose for a campsite. Up the road the stream went over a waterfall, its roar carrying down to the campsite.

Although it was only midafternoon, Vince halted the column, and the stagecoach swayed on its springs as it turned off the road. The three wagons loaded with baggage and supplies followed it, and the army wagon came behind them. When they all were in place, the servants climbed down while the drivers unhitched the horses. Vince dismounted and then helped Arabella down from her horse.

Once the servants had chosen a place for Arabella's tent, several of them erected it as others kindled a fire for her and her father. The shadows in the valley were long, and the crisp mountain air made the aged Don Raimundo's bones ache. As soon as a fire was built, Vince helped the grandee down from the coach and seated him comfortably beside it, wrapping a blanket around him. The old man grimaced and rubbed a bony shoulder.

"Are you feeling all right, Don Raimundo?" Vince asked when he noticed the grandee's expression.

"It is the chill of the night air, Captain. It causes my bones to ache."

This was the first time the old man had admitted to being in pain, and Vince and Arabella shared a look of concern. "We'll be crossing the crest of the mountain within a few days, sir," the captain stated. "After that, the temperature will be higher each day."

The grandee gave a cackling laugh. "I have much to look forward to then, Captain."

As the maids were rushing to build up the fire and fetch blankets for the grandee, Federico Murillo, the stolid foreign ministry official, stepped up and made one of his rare unsolicited comments. "You should take some of your laudanum, Don Raimundo," he suggested.

"Yes, you should, Father," Arabella agreed. "It will ease the pain. Shall I get it from the medicine chest?"

"I dislike using it, because it makes my mind dull," Don Raimundo mused, hesitating over the decision. Finally, he shook his head. "No. I would much rather read than spend hours in a cloud of opium. I will forgo the laudanum for now. If the pain is still this severe tomorrow, I will take some then."

Don Raimundo stayed near the fire as dinner was being prepared. Seeing he was well situated, Arabella and Vince strolled around the camp, stretching their stiff legs. As they neared a stream, Vince pointed toward it and said, "There are traces of gold in most of the streams in this region. Would you like me to show you how prospectors pan for gold?"

Arabella's dark eyes glistened as she said, "Oh, yes, Vincent. I would enjoy that very much."

After they had returned to the campsite to get a wide, shallow pan from the cook, they went back to the stream. Arabella watched with breathless anticipation

as Vince scooped up gravel from riffles to wash in the
pan. When sunset came, he had panned three small
nuggets and one fairly large one, all of which he gave to
Arabella.

She was thrilled, and Vince smiled at the sophisticated young woman's childlike nature. The matching
earrings, necklace, and brooch she wore contained
many ounces of gold as well as many carats of diamonds,
but she seemed to consider the fractional ounce of gold
in her palm more precious.

"I am very grateful you found this for me, Vincent,"
she said, moving the nuggets on her palm with a finger-
tip.

"I'm sure we can find more along the way, but it's
getting dark, so we'd better go back to the camp,"
Vince said.

Arabella nodded, and together they walked back to
join the others.

The fires blazing up at the campsite cast a warm,
cheerful glow in the gathering darkness. The drivers
and the soldiers not on sentry duty were cooking at one
fire, the servants at another. At the third fire, where
Don Raimundo sat, the cook was preparing a delicious,
abundant spread for dinner, as usual. Several of the
servants were accomplished musicians, and as the food
was being prepared and served, they strummed Spanish songs on their guitars near the fire where the grandee sat.

Vince and Arabella joined Don Raimundo. During
the meal the young woman said, "I do not know that I
ever will want to return to Spain. America is becoming
like home to me. And there is so much more to see."

Looking up at the stars, Vince sadly reflected that the
time would inevitably come when she would be gone.
He had finally met the woman he loved and wanted to
make his wife, and marriage seemed beyond the realm
of possibility.

Chapter Eight

Looking up at an eagle as it rode the air currents on stilled wings, Billy Carlson envied its ability to speed across miles in a soaring, graceful glide. At fifteen, he found life on a small ranch in the eastern foothills of the Los Piños Mountains very confining and at times boring.

The nearest neighbors were far to the north, a distance that took five days of hard traveling to cover. The only break in the monotony was when cattle were driven north to be pooled with those from other small ranches and taken to the market in Albuquerque. Whenever he had the time, Billy pored over the stack of old, tattered magazines in the house and dreamed of the day when he could go to a big city and see the things pictured on the torn pages.

At one side of the ranch was a narrow road, which seemed to Billy to lead nowhere. In one direction it stretched down to the dry, lifeless flatlands, and in the other it wound through the foothills to the deserted wilderness of the mountains. At times he looked at the road and dreamed that it was broad and well traveled, with houses on either side.

"Billy!" his father called to him from the corral. "Are you daydreaming again?"

"No, sir," he replied. "I was just looking at the eagle."

"Well, go look for your mother's milk cow instead," his father said, a tolerant smile on his bearded face. "It's roamed off for the second time today, probably into the woods. Take your rifle, and do it soon."

As he walked to the small house for his rifle, Billy reflected that finding the milk cow was usually a task for either his sister, who was nine, or his brother, who at eight was the youngest of the children. But then he realized that he was being sent for the same reason that his father had reminded him about his rifle: During the past two days his father had suspected that Indians were lurking about. While they had never done more than steal a few cattle, it was wise to take precautions.

In the kitchen his mother was starting to make stew for dinner, and her smile at Billy had an anxious edge as he took down his rifle from the pegs beside the door. He tucked it under his arm, went back out, and then crossed the field at the side of the house, walking slowly into the forest. Stepping around the trees, he listened for the cow's bell.

Only a little time had passed when Billy stopped to listen more closely, thinking he had heard hoofbeats in the distance. Immediately he thought about what his father had said about Indians, and he wondered if they were trying to take the milk cow or any of his father's herd. But it was barely after midday, and they had always come at night to steal cattle. He cupped a hand behind his ear and turned his head from side to side, but he could hear nothing over the rustle of the trees in the breeze. Dismissing it, he walked on.

Suddenly he heard the boom of his father's Winchester, instantly followed by another shot. Turning, the youth raced back toward the ranch. Other shots rang out as Billy, panting from fear and exertion, threw all his strength into his legs. After a moment the gunfire stopped, followed by an ominous silence. He struggled to keep up his pace, but he felt himself slowing.

At a hundred yards from the edge of the trees, his breathing a hoarse rasping in his ears, Billy heard savage, triumphant whoops. Then his mother screamed, a sound that touched something deep within him. With that he found new strength, and his footsteps were light as he raced through the woods.

He burst out of the forest, sliding to a stop. Numbed beyond horror, he looked at the four silent forms on the ground in front of the house. Indians danced around them, whooping as they waved their bloody weapons and scalps. One Indian stood to the side, calmly watching the others. In their brutal, bloodthirsty glee, none of them noticed Billy.

His lungs laboring for air, he controlled his breathing to steady the rifle as he shouldered it. Lining it up on one of the Indians dancing about, Billy held his breath and squeezed the trigger. The rifle bounced as it fired, and when Billy looked up, he saw the Indian falling to the ground. The other Indians peered about with sudden consternation, then scattered. Billy worked the lever and fired at an Indian racing for cover, but the bullet missed the target, kicking up dirt beside the man.

The other attackers took cover at the front of the house behind a wood pile. They raised their bows and shot blindly around the corner, and the arrows thudded into the ground around Billy as he aimed at the house, waiting. He glimpsed a head and fired, and splinters exploded from the logs. The Indian crawling toward cover in front of the house was only wounded, but he was too close to the lifeless forms of Billy's family, so the boy did not shoot.

Billy did not see that an Indian had run all the way around the house to the rear corner until a well-aimed arrow was already in the air. He heard more than felt it penetrate his stomach, a heavy thud with little pain, but the impact pushed him backward. The Indian, racing into the meadow, whooped in triumph but then hid in the deep grass as Billy shakily got to his feet. He held his rifle at waist level and snapped off a shot.

Backing into the trees, the boy staggered as weakness seized him and pain began to throb in his stomach. The Indians at the front of the house darted into the meadow and took cover in the grass, then crawled toward Billy. He leaned against a tree and fired at the movements. Then the hammer snapped on an empty chamber.

In desperation, Billy used a tactic that had been handed down through generations of settlers. He hurled the rifle as far out into the deep grass as he could, delaying the Indians while they found it. Then he ran to hide in the forest.

He had difficulty breathing and the pain in his stomach had become searing when he reached a large deadfall. As he ducked under the mass of dead, rotting limbs and brush that surrounded the fallen tree, he grasped the arrow and moaned in agony. Almost fainting from the excruciating pain, he fell to the ground and lay still.

He heard the Indians calling to one another, and then there were footsteps and hoofbeats pattering back and forth. He heard them tearing another deadfall apart. Then one of the Indians shouted in a stern, commanding voice. Hoofbeats drummed, and there was silence.

After a time Billy crawled out of the deadfall, dazed with pain, his breath catching in his throat. Through the tops of the trees, he saw smoke billowing up from the house, and he knew that his mother, father, brother, and sister were dead—and that the same fate was about to befall him.

It was late in the afternoon when Vince Bolton reached the crest of a hill and lifted his arm to stop the column. He saw smoke rising a few miles down the road. Arabella noticed it at the same time and asked, "What do you think it is, Vincent?"

"It's difficult to be certain. You stay right beside the sergeant while I find out, Arabella. I mean it."

"Of course, Vincent."

He turned to the sergeant, who had ridden forward. "Pick out five men to go with me, and I'll see what's burning there, Sergeant Henshaw. Take command here and continue traveling down the road. If there's any danger ahead, I'll send word back."

The sergeant reined his horse around and called out five names, beckoning the men forward. As they rode up to Vince, he smiled at Arabella and touched his hat, nudging his horse with his spurs. His smile faded as he led the men away; he feared he knew what was burning down the road.

When he had last been in this area, years before, there had been no houses within many miles. However, on many occasions when he had led a troop in response to a reported Indian attack, the smoke from a burning house had guided him to the scene. The smoke billowing up down the road looked just like what he had seen those times.

After half an hour of riding at a rapid canter, Vince's fears were confirmed. He reined up in front of the house, noticing at once the bodies in front of the smoldering timbers. Blood was on the ground not far from the bodies, possibly from a wounded Indian. In front of the house were ammunition boxes that had apparently been carried outside and cast away after being hastily emptied. Vince noted the type of caliber and the ammunition, then picked up several arrows and examined them closely to make certain all of them were Mescalero.

He turned to one of the soldiers. "Ride back and tell Sergeant Henshaw that there's been an Indian attack here and that under no circumstances do I want the women to see this. I want him to turn off the road and make camp beside the brook."

Looking across the field beside the house, he saw trampled-down patches in the deep grass and arrows in the ground at the edge of the trees. He summoned the soldiers and told two of them to search the forest. "The Indians were shooting at someone over there," he said. "You might find another body in the woods. I'm sure the Indians are long gone now, but keep your eyes open anyway."

The soldiers rode away, and as he turned to the other two, Vince saw that one of them had moved aside and was vomiting after having seen the bodies. His name was Jessup, and at seventeen he was the youngest soldier in the party. Vince turned to the other one. "When Trooper Jessup gets finished there, you two look for tools in the barn. If you find any, pull some boards loose and start making coffins."

In the pasture behind the corral and barn, Vince saw where the Indians had approached the house. Examining the footprints, he figured out how many there had been and then rode to the forest far back from the pasture and found where their horses had been left.

A few head of cattle had been driven away to the north, but many more were standing about in the pasture. As Vince rode back toward the house, one of the soldiers who had gone into the forest appeared, riding at a fast canter. "We found a boy, Captain Bolton," he called. "He's got an arrow in him, but he's still alive."

Vince followed the soldier, who led him to the deadfall in the forest. A few yards from it, the other soldier was kneeling over the boy. Vince dismounted and went to him. He was semiconscious, and Vince could see right away that he had little or no chance of recovering. The arrow through his stomach had penetrated vital organs.

After cutting the feathered butt off the arrow, Vince carefully pulled out the shaft. Looking briefly at the feathered section, he pocketed it and then took the youth in his arms, cradling him. He carried the boy back to the ranch and put him in the shade beside the house. A soldier followed with Vince's horse and then went to the springhouse at the captain's order. A minute later he returned with a dipper of cold water, which Vince poured slowly into the boy's mouth until he regained consciousness.

In a hoarse, breathless whisper, the boy told Vince his name and those of his family. Then he described what he had seen. "I sure wish you had got here a little sooner . . ." he finished, sighing.

"So do I, Billy. I've never regretted anything more in my life."

The soldier gave Billy another sip of water, and then the youth groaned, his face twisting in agony. Hearing the wagons, coach, and teams, Vince turned and saw that they were moving off the road toward the brook. He told Billy that he would return soon with something for his pain, and ordering the soldier to remain with the youth, he left.

Vince mounted his horse and rode toward the campsite. The sergeant met him at the road, and when Vince had dismounted and they were walking to where the others were setting up camp, he related the fate of the family and the evidence he had found. "They seem to be one of White Eagle's foraging parties, although what they've done doesn't fit his pattern," he explained. "There are about a dozen of them. It looks like at least one was wounded. Most of them are armed with bows and arrows, but a few must have had firearms. They took more guns from the farmhouse, along with ammunition."

"Are you sure they're White Eagle's warriors, sir?" Henshaw asked. "I thought he never went beyond stealing livestock."

Vince stopped walking and pulled the feathered butt of the arrow from his back pocket and held it up. "This was the arrow that injured the boy. All the others scattered around near him were the same."

Henshaw took the arrow and shook his head. "That's White Eagle's, all right. I wonder what's made him start slaughtering settlers."

"I don't know, Sergeant. It's possible that he didn't give the order for this to take place, though. He could have a rogue warrior among his leaders. The warriors who did this left heading north instead of toward the main camp in Mexico. And they left cattle standing all over the place, and that's not like White Eagle's foraging parties, either."

"Neither is raiding during the daytime."

"You're right." The captain was silent for a moment, and then he said, "If one of White Eagle's leaders *is* defying him, it could mean trouble for us. Normally we could handle them with our troop, but we have people to protect. That puts us in a defensive position and at a disadvantage."

"It does, sir. I'll tell the troops to be alert every minute."

The two men started toward the campsite again, and as they neared it, Vince said, "Take some men over to the ranch to dig graves and help build coffins. And I'd like some laudanum for that lad over there. I understand Don Raimundo has a bottle of it."

Word that some carnage had taken place at the ranch had already spread through the party of travelers, but Arabella and her father were horror-struck when Vince related the extent of the massacre. As soon as the captain mentioned the youth who was in pain, Arabella rushed to get the laudanum from the medicine chest.

"I wish there was more we could do to help," Don Raimundo said. "*Surely* there is something."

"No, there's nothing anyone can do," Vince told him. "The lad doesn't have long to live, I'm afraid, but at least the laudanum will ease his pain."

Breathlessly, Arabella returned with the bottle and asked, "Where is the boy, Vincent?"

"No, Arabella. I don't want you seeing—" Vince began, but she turned away and ran across the road. Vince called out to her, but she had already spotted the boy near the house, and she ran quickly to him, with Vince following. When she reached the lad, she knelt down and cradled his head in her lap.

As Vince drew up and knelt beside her, he reflected that Arabella's reaction to the crisis was impressive. With admiration in his eyes, he watched her give Billy two deep drinks from the bottle of laudanum.

"He is in much pain, Vincent," Arabella said, her dark eyes shining with tears. "What can we do?"

"That should ease the pain some, Arabella. There's not much more we can do."

Murillo, who had followed them to the boy, was standing behind them, and Vince looked up in surprise as the official spoke.

"I will take the laudanum back to the medicine chest, if you wish." Murillo stepped toward Vince and held out a hand for the bottle. "I have seen more than enough of the tragedy here. I am going back to the camp."

Thinking that the murders had made even the foreign ministry official want to be helpful, the captain handed the bottle to him.

When Vince turned his attention back to Billy, the boy's pain seemed to be increasing, despite the laudanum. He was writhing in agony and, after a few minutes, began thrashing about. The convulsion was soon over, and then the boy was still.

"He's dead, Vincent!" Arabella exclaimed after feeling for a pulse. Tears glistened in her eyes as she looked up at the captain. "He went so quickly."

Vince's brow was furrowed with puzzlement. "I didn't think there was much hope, but I did expect him to last longer than that."

"Oh, Vince, he was so young. . . ." As Arabella wept, Vince put his arm around her and stroked her black hair. Softly he said, "You did the best you could, Arabella. Come. Let's go back to the others." She was sobbing as he helped her up and walked her slowly to her father.

Don Raimundo put his arm around his daughter and shook his head sadly. "At least he is in peace now, my dear. You did all you could for him."

Vince left the two alone and went to help set up the campsite.

Later that evening, when the coffins had been built and everyone had eaten, Vince went to his belongings and took out his Bible. As he walked to the newly dug graves with Don Raimundo, Arabella, and Murillo, the servants and soldiers followed, carrying lanterns. At the gravesite, the group gathered on opposite sides, the soldiers standing in formation. At the head of the graves, Vince read a passage from the Bible and said a prayer. When the brief service was finished, the group silently returned to the camp and bedded down for the night.

The next few days proved thankfully uneventful for the large group of travelers, and a sense of relief passed among the Americans and Spaniards alike. They had crossed the highest point of their journey and were coming down the other side of the Los Piños. As they prepared their camp in the evening after a beautiful day, a sense of celebration pervaded the group, and the evening meal proved to be more like a party than the other meals had been.

After Vince had assisted Don Raimundo into his wagon for the night and seen that Arabella and the others were safely in their tents, he stretched out in his bedroll near a fire. The stars were shining brightly above him with only a few clouds blocking their brilliance. It was not long before he dozed off.

Only an hour or two had passed when Vince woke suddenly and sat up in his blankets, every sense keenly alert. The camp was quiet under the bright moonlight shining down on the wide, sandy valley the column had reached at sunset, and all seemed right. But Vince knew he had been awakened by something that was a signal of potential danger.

A moment later it came again, and he realized it had been a noise. A whisper of thunder carried across the distance from far to the north. He waited, listening, and when he heard it once more, it sounded closer. The moon and stars were still bright, but a thunderstorm spawned in the mountains to the north was moving southward toward them.

Vince knew that in the downpour of a thunderstorm the dry valley where they were camped would become a riverbed of raging flood waters, coursing down through arroyos on the adjacent hills. Pushing his blankets aside, he reached for his boots and tunic. "Sergeant Henshaw!" he called.

The sergeant awoke with a snort on the other side of the dying embers of the fire. "Yes, sir?" he replied.

"A thunderstorm is headed this way. Let's get everyone moved to higher ground."

"Yes, sir!" the sergeant barked, and then he bellowed at the men, "Wake up and get a move on! We're breaking camp! Sentries, start sorting out the horses so we can get saddled up!"

The camp came alive in the night, the men scrambling from their bedrolls and moving about in a babble of sleepy voices. Vince rolled up his blankets and called to Arabella in her tent, waking her. Then he went to the wagon where Don Raimundo was sleeping to wake him.

The thunder moved closer rapidly, and the breeze that had made the campfire ashes glow suddenly became a gusty wind as the stir in the camp turned into pandemonium. Soldiers hastily saddled their horses, and drivers hitched up their teams. Vince helped Don Raimundo into the coach, and Arabella pulled on a cloak over her nightgown as Vince also led her into the coach.

By the time the column was ready to move out, the thick clouds were turning the night into an inky darkness that was broken only by the intermittent blinding glare of lightning. The headlamps on the stagecoach and wagons glowed through the choking sand and dust being whipped up by the buffeting wind. As Vince led the way across the valley, a shower of stinging hailstones fell, making the horses buck and plunge. Then the first large, heavy drops of rain thudded into the ground.

The full fury of the thunderstorm came in a barrage of lightning and thunder. The rain turned into a downpour, lashed by the howling wind first in one direction and then in another. The ground was unable to soak up the deluge fast enough, and within minutes the horses and vehicles were splashing through several inches of water. Then the runoff from higher ground began to course into the valley, and by the time the column neared a hill, the water was rising rapidly.

The hill was a steep one, and lightning gleamed on the sheet of water that was pouring down it. Vince took the rope from his saddle and reined up beside the coach as he called out orders: "Sergeant Henshaw, have the men help get the wagons up the hill! You men there, help with the coach!"

Nearby soldiers moved toward the coach as the sergeant barked orders to the others, and Vince leaned over to tie the end of his rope to a brace under the box. As Culley stood in the box, cracked his whip, and shouted at the teams, the soldiers pulled up alongside the coach and tied their ropes. Then the horses broke into a gallop, picking up speed for the hill.

As the stagecoach started up, it tilted precariously from side to side, its wheels sinking and the horses sliding in the mud. Vince kept the rope to his saddle horn taut, using the reins to keep his horse from falling. In the melee of plunging horses, Culley bellowed and cracked his whip, while the stagecoach slowly made headway up the slippery hill.

Behind the stage, servants were shrieking in fright as the wagons skidded and teetered, their drivers cracking whips and shouting at the teams. The lanterns on the wagons were lost in the downpour, and the headlamps on the coach were only occasionally visible through the heavy rain. The vehicle itself was only a thicker shadow in the dark night, with the vague forms of soldiers moving around it.

Near the coach Vince glimpsed a man silhouetted momentarily against the headlamp. He was not wearing a wide-brimmed campaign hat, as the soldiers did, and he seemed to be dismounting beside the stage-coach. He got too close to the horses, who were struggling for footing, and as a heavy hoof struck him, he cried out in pain.

In Vince's opinion the man's behavior approached the insane and put him at the dire risk of being run over by the coach in the darkness. He shouted to a soldier, "You there, trooper! Whoever that is beside the coach, get him back on his horse and away from the coach!"

The soldier reined his horse toward the coach. With one less man on that side to help with a rope, the coach teetered even more. Vince concentrated on keeping the rope to his saddle horn taut and his horse on its feet in the mud. A moment later the soldier rejoined the others. Lightning flashed just then, illuminating the face of the man who had been beside the coach as he rode away from it. It was Federico Murillo.

Finally the coach, with the wagons following it, reached a broad, level shoulder of the hill. When the vehicles stopped, Vince dismounted, untied his rope from the coach, and then stepped to the door. Opening it, he looked in at Arabella and her father, dimly illuminated by a small wall lamp. "I'm very sorry for all the jolting," he said. "I trust you're all right."

Both of them seemed unruffled by the wild ride up the hill, and Don Raimundo nodded. "We are unharmed—and very grateful for an escort who recognizes impending dangers! Come in from the rain and sit with us, Captain."

"Thank you, but I must check on the others. Murillo may have been injured. Try to rest, because it'll be dawn soon. The storm should end by daybreak."

Closing the door, Vince stepped to his horse and mounted. The lightning had moved on to the south, and the rain tapered off as he went to each wagon and checked on the people inside. The servants who were huddled under the canvas covers were unnerved by what had happened, but none of them had been injured.

The soldiers kindled a fire under an overhang at one side of the level expanse, and once it was going, they made coffee. Vince joined them, and as he stepped up to the fire, he saw Murillo among the drivers and soldiers. "Were you injured back there, Señor Murillo?" he asked.

The man's eyes fluttered open, and he moaned as he focused on Vince. "My leg . . . my leg is bruised, Captain Bolton."

"Are you in pain?" Vince asked. "We could get the laudanum. I'm sure Don Raimundo would not object."

"No, I . . . I will be all right," Murillo murmured, his eyes showing panic. "There is no more laudanum. I dropped the bottle." Murillo winced with pain and then looked up at Vince again and said quickly, "I hope Don Raimundo will not be angry at me."

Vince stood up. "If it was an accident, he has no reason to be angry. I'll ask Don Raimundo if you can ride in his wagon." The captain turned to leave, but then he looked back at the Spaniard and said, "By the way, Señor Murillo, what were you doing, riding so close to the stagecoach that way? It was a very dangerous thing to do."

Murillo closed his eyes as he answered, "I wanted to get the stagecoach up the hill, as the soldiers were doing, but I fell off my horse."

"Well, you're lucky you didn't get hurt worse. I hope you're feeling better soon."

As he went to ask Don Raimundo's permission for Murillo to ride in his wagon, Vince thought about what the foreign ministry official had said. The man had appeared to dismount rather than fall, but Vince figured he could have been wrong, and there was no obvious reason why Murillo would have dismounted. Nevertheless, Murillo had always seemed to be a very capable rider—but, Vince countered, mishaps could happen to anyone. Dismissing the matter, Vince talked with Don Raimundo about Murillo for a few minutes and then moved away toward Henshaw.

The sergeant told Vince that some of the soldiers had dropped their bedrolls and other items of equipment while getting the wagons up the hill. "Helping with the coach and wagons is no excuse, of course," Henshaw added. "If their equipment had been secured properly, they wouldn't have dropped it."

"No, they wouldn't have," Vince agreed. "If this were a regular patrol and they had to leave hurriedly in the middle of the night to chase after Indians, they wouldn't have a chance to recover what they lost. Have them gather up the things they dropped at first light. And give them instructions on securing their equipment at the first opportunity."

Nodding, the sergeant moved away to talk with the soldiers. Vince poured himself a cup of coffee and sipped it as he looked out into the darkness from the shelter of the overhang. As he watched, the rain seemed to fade to isolated drops.

The storm was completely past when dawn came, and the flood in the valley was subsiding. As the sun rose, it made the lingering clouds glow in a rage of reds and yellows, while rainbows arched against the sky far to the south. Vince helped Don Raimundo from the stagecoach, and as the older man dressed for the day, the servants built a fire, and the soldiers who had dropped items of equipment went to look for them.

As the soldiers prowled about on the muddy hill, finding their things, a young recruit came over to Vince and handed him a dagger. "One of the men found this, Captain Bolton," he said. "Someone in the party we're escorting must have dropped it coming up the hill."

Examining the dagger, Vince saw that it was of Spanish manufacture, made of Toledo steel. An expensive weapon, its gleaming blade was razor-sharp, and its ebony handle was inlaid with gold and silver. It was also a puzzle, because as far as Vince knew, none of the Spaniards was even armed, much less carrying a weapon like a dagger.

When Don Raimundo had finished dressing, Vince stepped over to him and asked if the dagger was his. Shaking his head, the grandee expressed the same perplexity that Vince had felt; as far as the aged man knew, no one in his party was even armed. In order to make certain, Vince went to each of the Spaniards with the dagger, but none of them recognized it.

The last one was Murillo, who seemed to be feeling much better. He shook his head when shown the dagger. "A government official's weapon is a pen, Captain Bolton, not a dagger. No, it is not mine."

Vince returned to the sergeant, and as he handed the dagger back, he shrugged. "I guess it doesn't belong to anyone, Sergeant Henshaw, so we certainly have a mystery, don't we?"

"Yes, sir," Henshaw agreed. "I suppose somebody else could have come this way and dropped it. It looks new, but it would take a long time for steel this good to tarnish out here in the drylands."

"Put it with the equipment in the wagon, and if we can't find an owner by the end of the journey, the man who found it can have it."

The sergeant nodded and turned away as Vince went to join Don Raimundo at his fire. The maid served coffee to them, and while Vince and the grandee discussed the hectic rush through the darkness to get out of the valley, Don Raimundo commented that Arabella would have many interesting, exciting memories to last her when she settled down to married life in Spain.

He spoke of her marriage as though it were a foregone conclusion, Vince thought. On another occasion when the Duke of Valencia had come up in a discussion between the grandee and Vince, Don Raimundo had mentioned that the duke's father was a political ally and close friend of his.

"I'm sure Arabella will be an excellent wife for him if she decides to marry him," Vince remarked grudgingly, forcing himself to say the right thing. "He will be an extremely fortunate man."

"His life will not be dull," Don Raimundo replied, smiling whimsically. "Like his father, he is inclined to be studious rather than active. His quiet routine of life will be upset, but I am sure he expects that."

Vince had learned that while the aged man permitted his daughter wide latitude in what she did from day to day, she trusted her father's judgment implicitly and followed his advice on important issues. His permission was a prerequisite to her marrying anyone, and it appeared definite that she was destined to return to Spain and marry the duke.

In his fantasies Vince had entertained hopes that Arabella might at least consider marriage with him—despite his knowing that it was unlikely—and that he could persuade her father to give his permission. The conversation depressed him, convincing him that his chances were minimal. He knew that Don Raimundo liked him as a friend, and it seemed at least possible that he was gently warning Vince away from any such ideas.

Concealing his disappointment, Vince continued talking when Arabella joined them. Having changed into an ivory-colored dress, gloves, and a hat with a veil to protect her from the sun, she was even more animated than usual that morning. She pointed out the wildflowers, which always reacted quickly to moisture and bloomed in a brilliant riot of color. Desert willow was in blossom along the washes, and its pleasant aroma wafted from the violet-scented flowers. The rocky slopes were covered with desert marigolds and flowering thistles, while the hilltops were solid beds of nama, wild heliotrope, and other colorful flowers.

While Vince remained dejected within, it was impossible for him to act moody when he was with Arabella. Her buoyant, vivacious personality was a sure antidote for his low spirits. He was determined to enjoy their time together as much as possible.

Chapter Nine

Captain Vince Bolton led the caravan at a slower pace once it left the road to travel over the rugged terrain of the flatlands. The sun glared down from a brassy, cloudless sky, and the torrid heat of the afternoon settled like a stifling blanket. Activity among the animals in the arid wasteland ceased, with the occasional chatter of a cicada the only sign of life. During the afternoon, rising heat waves from the terrain shortened the horizon to a shimmering blur, limiting visibility. While it provided excellent cover for the caravan, Vince knew it could also be used against them. He had the uneasy feeling that it was being used against them now. Several times since they had left the mountains behind he thought he had seen dust being raised a mile or so behind the column. Since the dancing heat waves created the illusion of movement in all directions, he had been uncertain then, but this afternoon he was absolutely sure he saw a wisp of dust behind.

When they made camp that evening, Vince discussed it with the sergeant. "It could have been a dust devil," he said, "although there wasn't much wind to stir one up. I could be wrong, but I believe it was horses."

"Maybe it was one of White Eagle's foraging parties taking a look at us," Sergeant Henshaw suggested. "I don't see how they could follow us for long, though, since we're so far from water. We're carrying all we need, but riders can't carry water for their horses."

"Their leader might be using that as a tactic to force his men to attack us," Vince mused. "We have water, and they need it. It would be hard on his horses and men, but he might push them to their limit to get it."

"That's true," Henshaw agreed. "I'll tell the men to stay especially alert when they're on sentry."

"There's one thing we can do that might help us," Vince said. "Have the men gather large bundles of dried grass, and tell them to keep matches on hand when they're on sentry duty. If we're attacked, they can light the bundles and throw them out from the perimeter. They'll be better able to see the Indians if they ride in."

Henshaw nodded. "I'll have the men gather grass right away, Captain Bolton. It sounds like you came up with some good ideas in the Arizona Territory regiment."

Vince smiled. "Yes, but we had good reason. Dealing with Geronimo stimulates hard thinking about new and different tactics to use."

The sergeant laughed, saluting as he walked away. Vince looked around at the campsite, which was on a level hill with virtually no natural cover. Not for the first time he reflected that the situation would be simple if he had only a patrol. Then, if he suspected Indians were following, he could merely wheel the patrol around and chase the Indians down. But in his present situation, with so many civilians to guard, all he could do was wait to see what happened.

The attack came two nights later. A rifle's blast broke the silence, and arrows arced at the sentries on the northern perimeter of the camp. As the soldiers began firing rapidly and shouting the alarm, Sergeant Henshaw leapt from his bedroll and bellowed orders. The men scrambled from their blankets and raced toward the northern perimeter, while sentries all around the edge of the camp lighted the bundles of grass and heaved them out into the darkness.

From his experience in battle, Vince knew that the single rifle fire and the small number of arrows coming from the north did not constitute a concentrated attack. He decided it was a ruse to draw the soldiers to that side of the camp; the main attack would come from the south, the side where the horses were picketed.

"Sergeant Henshaw!" he shouted. "Send the first squad to support the sentries on the southern perimeter of the camp."

"Yes, sir!" the sergeant replied. "First squad, get to the southern perimeter on the double! Move!"

The men were silhouetted against the burning grass as they followed Vince across the camp. At that instant, three rifles blazed from the darkness to the south, accompanied by a hail of arrows, creating a panic among the horses. Even the trained cavalry mounts were frightened by the gunfire since they were not controlled by riders, and they whinnied and reared up against the picket rope.

Suddenly the gunfire and arrows were concentrated on the west side of the camp, and Vince glimpsed a movement there. Two Indians crouched low as they raced through the light from the burning grass, carrying only knives and heading toward the horses.

Shouting at the soldiers behind him, Vince pointed to the Indians. The two warriors dashed past the sentries on the west side of the camp, who were lying flat and taking cover from the rifle fire and arrows directed at them. Vince aimed his pistol, tracking the first Indian and waiting until the sentries were out of his line of fire, and then squeezed the trigger. The Indian fell, shot through the chest.

Swinging his pistol toward the second Indian, Vince fired again. The Indian, who was within a few yards of the picket line, staggered as the bullet struck him. In a last, long stride, he made it to the rope and slashed it with his knife as he fell. The horses, in a frenzy from the gunfire, exploded in all directions. They headed pell-

mell toward the darkness, fleeing the pandemonium
that had frightened them.

Vince holstered his pistol as he raced after the horses,
shouting at the soldiers to catch them. He managed to
seize the halters of two of them, though the frightened
animals jerked him in opposite directions before he
managed to calm them. The sentries caught several
more, and one was stopped as it ran toward the northern side of the camp. But the vast majority of the animals fled into the night.

Their attack a success, the Indians whooped in triumph as they chased the runaway horses. In the aftermath of the battle, the stage driver, Culley, and the
wagon drivers gathered around the handful of horses,
estimating their loss. After the final count was taken,
the news spread quickly that only seven had been
saved.

Vince left the others to check on Arabella and her
father. The grandee had climbed out of the wagon
where he slept to see about his daughter, and the two of
them were standing in front of her tent.

Don Raimundo smiled as Vince asked if they were all
right. "We are unharmed, Captain, with yet one more
incident in a very eventful journey to remember. Will
you be able to recover any of the horses?"

"I intend to, because we'll be in a difficult position
without them. I'm taking some men and going after
them now. Nothing more will happen here tonight, so
you should get your rest, if you can."

Arabella put a hand on Vince's arm and spoke softly,
"Please, Vincent, be careful."

He nodded as he turned away and walked across the
camp toward Henshaw. "Have those seven horses saddled up, Sergeant," he said, "and pick out five men to go
with us. Make sure they're well armed and tell them to
carry plenty of rope. We're going to recover the horses.
The remainder of the men are to be posted on sentry
duty."

Vince then studied the dead Indians near the picket

line. One had a crude buckskin bandage on his shoulder, and the other had a bandage wrapped around a splinted arm. Vince took out his knife and, kneeling beside the nearest one, cut away the bandage. It covered a bullet wound that was several days old. Probing with the knife, Vince found that the bullet was still in the wound, and he began to remove it.

Sergeant Henshaw stepped up to Vince and bent over, watching the procedure. "He's one of White Eagle's warriors, all right. The leader of that bunch is a cold-blooded bastard," he commented grimly, "using his wounded for a suicide mission."

Extracting the bullet, Vince wiped his knife on the ground and sheathed it. He stood up and examined the slug. "This Indian was wounded at the Carlson ranch. This is from a Winchester .44-40, the kind of rifle that Billy and his father were using."

Henshaw looked up at Vince. "Then you were right in what you thought at the ranch, Captain. White Eagle has a rogue leading warrior on the loose. He came after us to get our horses."

"Yes, it looks that way, and now we know more about him. He's cold-blooded all right, and he knows tactics, because his attack here was perfectly coordinated. I hate to say it, but we might be in danger of having another leader like Geronimo on the warpath." Tossing the bullet away, Vince turned toward the seven remaining horses. "The Indians should have our other horses rounded up by now, so we'll have a good trail to follow. Let's get going."

Once Vince saw that camp was secure, with the other soldiers surrounding it, he went to the horses, where the five men were mounted and ready to ride, their carbines and supplies loaded onto their saddles. Vince and Sergeant Henshaw stepped into their saddles and checked their weapons, and then the group rode out of camp.

Leading the six men in the bright moonlight, Vince made a wide circle around the camp, looking for hoofprints. A short time later he found prints where the Indians had rounded up some of the horses. Noticing a broad path of hoofprints to the north of the camp that was easy to see in the moonlight, he followed it at a canter to a point some two miles to the west of the camp, where the horses appeared to have been driven into an arroyo.

Leaving the sergeant and soldiers, Vince circled the ravine slowly and then returned to the sergeant. "They stopped here to put halter ropes on the horses," he said. "Then they went on to the west, each Indian leading several horses. But I don't think they'll continue in that direction. I think it's a trick. The nearest water to the west is in the foothills, and those horses would never make it that far."

"I don't know of any water that's closer," Henshaw said.

"There's a spring called Manatial Lobo a little over twenty miles southwest of here. My guess is that the Indians will split up after a time as they ride to the west and try to lose us by making several trails. Then they'll rejoin and ride for Manatial Lobo."

Henshaw's mouth formed a humorless smile. "But we'll be there waiting for them."

"That's right. We'll ride straight south and approach the spring from below so we won't leave a trail for them to cross. I believe the leader of those Indians is too confident to stop and have the area scouted wide on his flanks, but I don't want to take any chances. You and the men ride single file behind me so we'll leave as little trail as possible."

The sergeant gave the soldiers the order and then followed as Vince rode away to the south. His horse cantering across the broken, rocky terrain in the moonlight, the captain tried to fix the location of the spring in his mind. The years that had passed since he had last been at that spot of greenery and water in this parched region made him unsure of its exact location, but he was confident that he would find it.

Hours later, his horse covered with sweat and panting from the hard pace, Vince turned to the west for several miles and then headed north. He slowed and searched the moonlit horizon carefully, not wanting to pass by the spring and leave hoofprints north of it. But his horse located it first. The thirsty animal smelled the water and tugged hard at the reins, trying to angle to the left.

Slackening the reins, Vince let the horse turn and pick its own way. In a matter of minutes he could see the trees around the spring silhouetted against the stars, and he could smell the water, a cool, fresh scent after the dusty odor of the flatlands. Reining the horse around, he led the soldiers to a ravine a hundred yards away and rode down into it.

Dismounting, Vince took a rope from his saddle. "Make certain your horses are tethered securely," he told the men quietly. "I don't want any of them breaking loose. We're going to spread out around the spring. I'll give each of you a firing position once we're up there. Don't move about or make a sound until the battle begins. I want those Indians to get close enough for us to take all of them, but I don't want any horses shot. I'll shoot first, and that will be your signal to fire."

His own horse tethered, Vince removed the carbine from its case at the side of his saddle. The men finished tying their horses and took out their weapons, then followed him from the ravine.

As they took their firing positions around the spring, wolves howled in the distance, a lonely, mournful sound in the night. Positioning himself so that he had an unobstructed view of the terrain to the north, Vince sat down behind a tree, and the long wait began. The brush and grass around the spring rustled, and a few thirsty creatures braved the scent of humans to approach it for a drink. A breeze stirred the trees, and then a line of light appeared on the eastern horizon. It dimmed the stars as it spread westward. When the sun rose, Vince saw a cloud of dust to the north.

The dust cloud rose higher, and soon Vince could

make out the horses and riders under it. Approaching at a canter, they closed the distance rapidly. He counted about a dozen Indians, and at a thousand yards he picked out the leader. The seconds passed slowly for Vince, and he urgently hoped none of the soldiers would move and show a gleam of sunlight on gun metal.

The lead Indian reined his horse back, causing the stolen animals that followed on halter ropes to slow down. Then he motioned for the other Indians to do the same. The mass of horses slowed to a trot, and the Indians peered warily at the spring. The leader, a tall half-breed, was the most cautious one; the others appeared satisfied that it was safe, but he held them back. Then, at five hundred yards, the horses scented the water.

Mad with thirst, several of them charged ahead. The Indians struggled to hold them, shouting as they jerked on ropes and beat the animals, but the horses had been too long without water, and their pace increased to a canter and then a run. Within seconds they were stampeding toward the spring, the Indians having lost all control over them.

Vince cocked his carbine and centered the bead on a warrior's chest, tracking the Indian as he moved. All the horses, even those that were mounted, thundered furiously toward the spring, foam flying from their lips. Vince waited for them to get within a hundred feet before tightening his finger on the trigger. When the carbine fired, the Indian fell, and suddenly gunfire roared all around the spring. Many of the Indians were shot and tumbled to the ground.

Frightened by the gunfire, the horses turned into a chaotic tangle, some still trying to get to the water while others attempted to flee. Dropping the halter ropes on the horses they were leading, the uninjured Indians recovered control over their mounts and began wheeling them around. Vince fired again, hitting another Indian, and then shot one more as he was riding away.

Three of the Indians got clear of the horses, lashing

their mounts and racing away, and one of them was the tall half-breed. The men around the spring continued firing rapidly, peeling one of the other two Indians from his horse.

Vince stood up and steadied his carbine against the tree, taking careful aim on the half-breed. He squeezed the trigger gently, but just as the carbine fired, the other Indian swerved his horse behind the half-breed's. The bullet struck him and made him reel, but he clung to his horse as he and the tall Indian disappeared over a low rise, turning to the south.

As the dust settled, it revealed the Indians scattered on the ground and nearly two dozen horses gulping down water. Other horses milled about, heading toward the spring as they overcame their fright from the gunfire.

"Sergeant Henshaw," Vince called, "have the men get those horses out of that water before they drink too much. When the horses are collected together, have graves dug for the enemy dead at a distance from the spring."

"Yes, sir," the sergeant answered. Then pointing to the horses the Indians had been riding, he added, "We got all of our horses back, plus nine more, Captain Bolton. Those nine extras are in poor condition, though."

"Yes, they are," Vince agreed, looking at the bony, mistreated horses. "With extra rations of grain and good care, they should improve very shortly." Vince looked toward the south. "The fact that two Indians got away doesn't bother me much, but I don't like it that one of them is the leader. He can cause us a lot of trouble."

"That big half-breed. But the way I see it, he might be in plenty of trouble himself, Captain. White Eagle has gone out of his way to avoid bringing the cavalry after him and his warriors, and that half-breed has undone all of that."

"Yes, but White Eagle won't feel very kindly toward a cavalry troop that virtually wiped out one of his foraging parties, regardless of the circumstances. He has a strong sense of justice." Returning to the task at hand, he said, "We'd better get back to the others. But first I'm going to join the horses in a good, long drink of water."

As his horse plodded southward at a slow walk, Dark Cloud seethed with anger. A carbine bullet had made a deep furrow across one side of his chest, and another had grazed his shoulder. The wounds twinged, but he scarcely noticed the pain as he writhed inwardly from the agony of having lost the horses, a prize that would have earned him prestige and admiration.

Fueling his rage was the realization that he had been deftly outwitted. He had considered his plan perfect, his escape with the horses assured. But his enemy had seen through his intentions, and his dream of glory had been shattered in the withering blast of carbines firing from ambush.

Having felt little more than contempt for his warriors, he was remorseful over their deaths only because it ruined his chances of being a leading warrior. After disobeying White Eagle's orders and getting his foraging party wiped out, he would be in disgrace. His hopes of becoming powerful and eventually replacing White Eagle would never be realized.

As his horse stumbled, Dark Cloud jerked the reins and drummed the animal with his heels. The horse tried to trot but then settled back into a slow, weary walk. It was almost exhausted, and without rest Dark Cloud knew it would probably never reach the main camp.

He glanced behind him at the warrior, who had a gaping wound in his upper chest where the last carbine bullet that had been fired had gone right through him. The wounded man was hunched over from pain and weakness, but he was stoically silent.

Looking at his last warrior, Dark Cloud suddenly thought of a solution to his difficulties. He could tell White Eagle that hunting had been very poor and he had approached the soldiers peacefully to ask for food, but they had attacked his party. His wounds would serve as proof that he had narrowly escaped death himself.

In addition to rescuing him from disgrace, Dark Cloud reflected, that solution would also be a means for revenge against the soldiers who had thwarted his plans. White Eagle would be enraged and would lead all of the warriors against the soldiers. But in order for the story to be believed, there could be no witnesses to contradict it.

Reining up beside a ravine, Dark Cloud dismounted. "We will stop here and rest for a time," he said.

The warrior lifted his head, his eyes glazed with pain. "Water," he whispered weakly.

"I will ease your thirst and your pain," Dark Cloud assured the man, helping him down from his horse.

The warrior smiled gratefully as he lay down near the edge of the ravine. His smile faded and his eyes opened wide when Dark Cloud took out his knife. Then his expression was transformed by shock and fear. He started to say something, but his words faded into a gasp as the long, sharp blade plunged into his heart.

Dark Cloud wiped his knife and pushed the body over the edge of the ravine, hearing it thump as it bounced down the steep wall and started a rock slide. He turned to his mount but then hesitated. The Winchester rifle tied on his horse was a prized possession, much better than his old one, but it would create questions. He could think of no explanation he could give White Eagle as to how he had obtained the rifle from the ranch.

With remorse—which he had failed to feel when killing the warrior—he tossed the Winchester into the ravine. Then he mounted his horse, leading the dead warrior's, and continued riding southward.

Chapter Ten

Three days after the Indian attack, the column was nearing Gran Quivira. Feeling a close connection with the ancient, deserted town because of their relative of centuries before, Arabella and her father were eagerly looking forward to seeing it. They never seemed to tire of hearing Vince tell them about his visits to the place.

The terrain to the east had a gentle upward slope that was no longer evident when the sun rose higher and the temperature increased, shortening the horizon to a blur of heat waves. But the slow upgrade was taking its toll, and the teams were sweating as they toiled over the low, sandy hills.

Late in the afternoon, the horizon ahead was no longer empty as Gran Quivira gradually emerged from the shimmering mass of heat waves. At first it looked to the people in the long column as though they were approaching a thriving town. The towering bulk of the mission church looked over a long row of buildings. But as the caravan got closer, the ravages of time became visible, and they saw that the town was inhabited only by the creatures of the arid wasteland.

The roof and part of the upper structure of the church had fallen in, and the walls of many of the houses were crumbling. The column passed ancient limestone quarries and fields marked with ridges, which revealed that orchards and crops had once grown there.

Vince led the way along a winding, debris-littered street to the large plaza facing the church. The wagons and stagecoach drew up to the west side of the plaza, where they would be shaded by the buildings.

As the sergeant ordered the soldiers to dismount, Vince stopped them. "Just a minute," he said. "You can see that many of the walls are unsafe, so be careful if you go looking around. Some of the buildings are like a maze, and it's possible to get lost in them—as well as crushed by falling adobe and stone. Most important of all, there are many rattlesnakes here. Watch where you're walking."

Vince helped Arabella down from her horse and then tethered their mounts. A few minutes later a comfortable camp had been made at the side of the plaza, and dinner was being prepared on the fires that were burning.

After everyone's hunger had been satisfied, Arabella and her father crossed the plaza to visit the church. Vince accompanied them to ensure that the structure was safe for them to enter. No trace of the front doors remained, but much of the rich, decorative carving on the thick beam above the entryway had endured through the centuries. As they entered the nave, Arabella and Don Raimundo crossed themselves. Vince shared their feeling that the ruined building remained a holy place. Dusk was falling, and he lit the two candles he had brought along, handing one to Arabella and one to her father.

Even in its state of decay, the church was a magnificent, impressive structure, some one hundred forty feet long, with walls that were six feet thick. Its former grandeur was especially evident in the peaceful, solemn ambience that was somehow immune to the ruin that the centuries had brought.

Sitting with Arabella on a block of masonry, Don Raimundo gazed at the church in the flickering light of the candles. "We have finally reached the place where our martyred relative went about his holy work, my daughter," he said quietly. "It more than fulfills my expectations."

"And mine, Father," she replied.

Leaving Arabella and her father alone, Vince went outside to order the soldiers to look for a water supply. After a time, when it became dark in the church, Arabella and her father emerged and blew out their candles. Vince and Arabella walked through the streets of ruin, and Arabella found a remnant of a basket that was similar to others she had found while crossing the flatlands. Vince shook his head when she asked him how old he thought it was. "I have no idea," he said, "but it could be several centuries old. It's so dry here that everything decays very slowly."

"Yes, I have noticed that and discussed it with my father. In many places even a skeleton will turn to dust in two hundred years, but not here. My father and I are very optimistic that when we find our martyred relative's remains, they will be intact." Arabella was silent for a moment and then continued, "The people who lived here once had ample water, orchards, crop fields, and all these houses. Why did they leave, Vincent?"

"They were peaceful farmers and artisans, Arabella," Vince explained as they walked along slowly in the diminishing light. "After the Pueblo revolt, the Spanish were gone for several years. With no soldiers here to protect the town, other Indians who were more warlike raided it so often that the inhabitants were finally driven away. Like Abo and Quarai to the north, the town has been deserted ever since then."

"How very sad, Vincent."

"Yes, it is. The people here were probably very happy at one time." He stopped walking and looked around. "It's getting late, Arabella. We'd better return to the plaza."

She glanced around regretfully as they turned back. "This place is so interesting, and we have seen hardly any of it. I would like to explore it thoroughly, Vincent. And the other two deserted towns as well."

The remark was a depressing one, for it reminded Vince that their time together was limited. It was similar to others she had frequently made, expressing a wish to stay in New Mexico Territory for an extended period. More than that, he reflected gloomily, he yearned to keep her with him for the remainder of their lives.

"Well, we won't go anywhere near Abo or Quarai," he said. "It would probably take weeks if not longer to explore this place thoroughly, and we'll leave here tomorrow morning."

Sighing with resignation, Arabella nodded. They talked about other things as they walked along the littered street, and when they were near the plaza, she suddenly laughed. "Vincent, when you told me that you have no romantic attachments, I found it difficult to believe. Now that I know you better, I can accept it readily."

Vince looked at her quizzically, asking, "What do you mean?"

"You said it yourself when you told me that you are married to the army. You are supremely skilled as a cavalry commander, but you are considerably less skilled in social subtleties."

"Well, it's true that I've spent far more time in a saddle than in parlors, but I'm still not sure what you mean. Have I done or said something to offend you? If I have, I sincerely apologize."

"No, no, of course not, Vincent. As my father said, you are a perfect gentleman. I was merely making an observation. . . ." Intentionally changing the subject, she said, "The stars always begin shining here before it is completely dark. That makes the twilight very beautiful, doesn't it?"

Still uncertain of what she had meant, Vince was curious and suspected that she was enjoying a private joke. "Yes," he answered. "But Arabella, I'm still not sure why you said that about me. Obviously I must have—"

"Vincent, please," she cut him off. "You have done

nothing to offend me. I should not have said what I did. I do not wish to speak of it any longer."

Since she had firmly dismissed the subject, their conversation moved on to other things while they walked back to the plaza. In the gathering darkness, the campfires were blazing. She and Vince joined her father at the fire where he was sitting, and the three discussed the trek to Chupadera Mesa—a short distance compared to what they had already traveled. It was also the only hard part of the journey that remained, since a road had been more or less cleared for the return trip to Socorro.

As he did each night, Vince saw that Arabella was safely in her tent before taking a lantern and accompanying Don Raimundo to the wagon where he slept. After helping the grandee up into the wagon, Vince stepped into it and hung the lantern under the canvas cover. Noticing that the bed was not as meticulously neat as the maid usually left it, Vince looked closer. "Wait just a minute, Don Raimundo. Something is wrong here," he said, taking the lantern down. Furrowing his brow, he held the lantern close to the bed as he nudged the mattress with his foot. The blankets seemed to move, and a slender bulge wriggled. When a muffled, clicking buzz came from under the blankets, Vince said quickly, "You must get down, Don Raimundo. Now! There's a rattlesnake in your bed."

"A rattlesnake . . ." the grandee murmured.

In the next instant Vince was assisting the elderly man down from the wagon. "You must stay well away from the wagon until I get rid of the snake," Vince told him. "And don't let anyone see you if you can help it."

"I am most grateful that you saw the snake, Captain," Don Raimundo said once he was on the ground. "I must search my bed each night for snakes, as I should have been doing all along. I have heard you warn the others repeatedly to do—"

"No, no," Vince interrupted, "you had no reason to look for snakes before now. You've heard me warn the others to check their bedrolls because they sleep on the ground, and snakes might crawl into their blankets with them. But a snake could never climb up one of the wheels and get in this wagon." He lifted the lantern higher, turning to face the grandee as they walked to a tree well away from the wagon. "Someone put that snake there, Don Raimundo. Someone tried to kill you."

The aged man was silent for a long moment, revealing no anger, dismay, or other emotion. He merely lapsed into deep thought, staring into space with those keen, youthful eyes that contrasted with his thin, wrinkled features. Then he slowly nodded. "So an enemy is trying to dispose of me," he murmured once they were at the tree. "I must try to find out who it is."

"It's got to be someone in your party, Don Raimundo."

The grandee shook his head as though amused. "If he is in my party, he is merely a tool, Captain. He must be stopped, of course, but the instigator is one of my enemies in Spain. Regretfully, I have several."

"Well, right now, I'd better get that snake out of your bed," Vince said, raising the lantern as he walked back to the wagon. "I'll get a forked stick so I can hold it still and shoot it."

"No, Captain! No one must know what you are doing," Don Raimundo said quickly. "The assassin must think that the snake crawled away and the attempt failed. If he knows we are aware of the attempt, it will be more difficult to set a trap to make him reveal his identity."

Impressed that the grandee was thinking so far ahead, Vince nodded as he searched for a stick near the wagon. The camp was quiet, but Vince knew that if the assassin were watching, there was nothing unusual about his moving about at night, because he often checked the sentries at irregular intervals.

Going to a small mesquite that had taken root in rubble near the wagons, Vince broke a limb from it and cleaned off the twigs to make a forked stick. He returned to the grandee's wagon and, climbing into it, hung the lantern to illuminate the bed. Cautiously he moved the blankets with the stick, and as the snake slithered into view, he pinned it, holding it firmly in place while he killed it with his knife. The snake writhed in its death throes as Vince tossed it into the ruins nearby. Then he returned to the tree where the grandee was waiting.

"It's safe now, Don Raimundo. Let me walk you back to the wagon."

The elderly man allowed Vince to take his arm, and as they walked back to the wagon, they quietly discussed who might have been responsible.

"It could be one of the servants," the grandee suggested, "because most of them are not old family retainers."

Vince looked closely at the old man's eyes and said softly, "Don Raimundo, do you recall how quickly young Billy died after he was given the laudanum?"

"Yes . . . but the poor child was mortally wounded, was he not?"

"Billy would most certainly have died, but I found it odd when he went into such violent convulsions immediately after we gave him the laudanum. Don Raimundo, I suspect that it was poisoned."

"Poisoned?" The old man was speechless for a moment. Finally, he said, "And who do you believe put the poison in the laudanum, Captain?"

Now it was Vince's turn to be quiet. He definitely had his suspicions. Throughout the journey Federico Murillo had shown no real affection for the grandee and his daughter, and the man's sour nature had done nothing to alter Vince's less than favorable impression of him. When Billy had died so quickly, Vince had thought it odd, but it was not until he learned that Murillo had dropped the bottle of laudanum that he truly suspected it was poisoned. And Federico Murillo had destroyed the evidence. . . .

Don Raimundo did not wait for Vince's response but

continued, "The one thing of which I am reasonably certain is that the assassin is motivated by greed. He is someone who will do anything for wealth, and we can use that insight to our advantage. Do you think the legends about the treasure of Gran Quivira are true, Vincent? Might we find items of immense value at Chupadera Mesa?"

"I believe it's likely that there's some basis for the legends," Vince answered. "As far as our finding anything, I can't predict that."

"If we do not find anything of material worth, we could make everyone believe we had found a treasure of such great value that we are reluctant even to let anyone see it. We could put rocks and branches in a bag and post one of the soldiers to guard it."

Vince smiled, nodding. "Yes, we could, and I think I know what you have in mind, Don Raimundo. If the assassin thinks we have something all that valuable, he'll do anything he can to get his hands on it."

"Yes, and flee with it. But before fleeing, he will attempt to assure himself of the reward he has been promised for killing me. So we are in the fortunate position of being able to guide his actions."

Vince agreed, and he and the grandee began to formulate a plan to trap the assassin. Don Raimundo had some reservations about it, because it would entail danger to Vince. But after some persuasion, Vince satisfied him that the risk was minimal. The quiet conversation continued until late in the night as they discussed the details of the plan.

The north face of Chupadera Mesa was a sheer rock cliff well over two hundred feet high and about a thousand yards wide. It rose so abruptly from the low, sandy hills and arroyos that it looked even larger, dominating the surrounding landscape. The bulk of the huge tableland reached back for almost a mile to where the southern end had eroded down into a steep, brushy slope with boulders scattered about it.

Although the caravan had safely reached its destination, Vince was well aware that they were by no means out of danger. If they were to be found on the mesa by Indians, the reaction to the desecration of their sacred place would be swift and violent. As they had traveled the last few miles to the mesa, he had scanned it through his binoculars while soldiers were deployed half a mile out on the flanks, looking for sign of Indians, but none had been spotted.

Vince led the column toward the northeast corner of the mesa, where a section of cliff weighing thousands of tons had fallen away aeons ago. The tall ridge of rock, some fifty feet from the base of the mesa, offered concealment for the stagecoach and wagons from any Indians who might pass at a distance. It was late afternoon when the column reached the mesa and the soldiers who had ridden wide on the flanks moved in to rejoin the troop.

As the wagons and stagecoach drew up in line alongside the towering rock, Vince turned to Henshaw and told him to keep two men on the rim of the mesa at all times as lookouts. "They're to report any sign of dust, fire, or anything else that could indicate Indians are nearby," he continued. "The north end of the mesa is the highest part, so post them there, and tell them to stay completely away from the ruins on the west side of the mesa. Those ruins are the part of the mesa that Indians regard as particularly sacred." Vince then announced that there would be no fires in the day when the smoke could be seen from a distance, and only small, concealed fires would be burned at night.

By the time night fell, a comfortable camp had been set up between the ridge of rock and the mesa. The horses were picketed at one side, and small, sheltered fires for cooking were kindled. Over dinner, Vince talked with Arabella and Don Raimundo about the way in which the search for the priest's remains would be conducted. He was clearly more concerned than they about the reaction of White Eagle's men if they were seen. He was having grave misgivings about bringing the Carranzas here.

Remaining confident about the outcome of the search, both Arabella and her father were enthusiastically anticipating it. She brought out the extracts she had made from Padre Eusebio's letters, and Vince looked through them once again as he talked with her and her father.

"In this sentence," Vince mused, "he mentions looking out toward the north, and Gran Quivira is north of here. He must have been situated on the northern rim of the mesa."

"Yes, that would seem to be true," Don Raimundo agreed.

"And here," Vince continued, turning to another page, "he refers to being protected from the elements and being comfortable while it was snowing. He must have had some sort of shelter up there."

"It must have been a well-constructed shelter," Arabella suggested. "If he was comfortable while snow was falling, the shelter had to be secure against the wind and have a fireplace. At least the walls of such a shelter would still be standing."

"Well, I'm not sure about that," Vince said doubtfully, handing the papers back to her. "Those mission priests endured hardships that most people would regard as torture. What he called comfortable, others might call just the opposite. We'll have to wait and see what we find up there. In several places he mentions having others with him. They must be the friars that you told me about, Don Raimundo."

"Yes," the grandee replied, "Fray Luiz Obregon and Fray José Toral. They were Padre Eusebio's faithful companions, accompanying him everywhere he went and sharing his privations and dangers. As I mentioned, they also failed to reach El Paso, and their fate is unknown. I am sure they went to their reward at the same time as Padre Eusebio, Captain, for they would never have left his side."

"And naturally," Arabella added, "we are obligated to have their remains interred in hallowed ground as well."

Her father emphatically seconded what she had said, and Vince ruefully reflected that their expectations were becoming more unrealistic as time went on. As he talked with them, he tried to temper their optimism to keep them from suffering severe disappointment, but to little avail. When the camp settled in for the night and Vince took Don Raimundo to the wagon where he slept, the grandee and his daughter were still just as confident.

The camp was stirring early the next morning. Breakfast was prepared before dawn, when the fires would have to be extinguished. At sunrise the sergeant posted guards at the camp, while Vince assisted Arabella up to her saddle and helped Don Raimundo onto a horse. They rode to the southern end of the mesa, followed by the remainder of the troop.

The horses filed up the steep, brushy slope to the top of the mesa, which was covered with sage and mesquite. It was the highest point for miles, and the surrounding countryside stretched out far in every direction. The soldiers dismounted at the northern end and waited while Vince looked around with Arabella and her father.

At the mesa's western side stood the ruins of the ancient village of stone houses. Peering at them, Arabella folded her arms and shrugged her shoulders, as if she were cold.

"Are you all right, Arabella?" Vince asked as he walked up beside her and Don Raimundo.

"I'm fine, Vincent," she answered. "Looking at these buildings just makes me feel eerie. Why do the Indians regard them as sacred?"

"According to ancient legends, the people who lived here were killed by a large raiding party from the mountains. But all of them—men, women, and children —fought with such courage that the raiding party was almost wiped out. Their spirits are said to linger here still, standing guard over their village, so the Indians avoid it and keep others away."

"By all means, we should respect the Indians' beliefs," Don Raimundo commented. "It is good that you have ordered everyone to stay as far from the ruins as possible, Captain."

"I've always made it a practice at least to try to show respect for the beliefs of Indians," Vince replied. Looking around uncomfortably, he added, "In a situation like this, it's difficult. We're already much too close to the ruins to satisfy them, but we should do the best we can under the circumstances."

Vince led the way along the northern edge of the mesa, zigzagging around the deep ravines that had been etched there over time by wind and rain. Some of them, choked with brush and boulders, reached over a hundred feet back from the rim. Arabella and Don Raimundo rode slowly behind him, all the while looking for evidence of a structure. It took a full hour for them to work their way to the west corner of the mesa.

"Perhaps the shelter would have been in one of the ravines for protection from the wind," Arabella suggested. "One can see that rock slides have occurred there, so the shelter could be covered up now. Locating such a buried shelter would require a close, careful search of the ravines."

"Yes, that's possible," Vince conceded. "I'll get the men started on a search for it."

They returned to the opposite corner of the mesa, and from there the wagons, stagecoach, horses, and people at the campsite looked very small far below. Vince divided the soldiers into two groups, telling them what to look for and warning them to be careful. "If you see a post with ax marks on it, it could be a roof beam or wall support. Also, look for any line of stones placed together. Be careful not to start rock slides in the ravines, and don't get too close to the edge. It's undercut in places and won't hold your weight."

As the men went to the ravines and climbed down into them to start searching, Vince turned to Sergeant Henshaw. "Take most of the horses back down to the camp for now. There's no point in keeping them saddled all day. Lunch will have to be brought up here, and I'd like to have a tent set up here, too, so Don Raimundo will have a comfortable place to rest now and then."

Henshaw looked at the aged man and smiled. "When I get to be that old, I hope I have as much sand in my craw as he does. He's as spry as a man of half his years."

"I've found out that he isn't physically strong, but he has tremendous willpower. He simply won't let himself give in to fatigue or the infirmities of age. I just don't want him to get too tired, because that could seriously affect his health."

The sergeant nodded in agreement, and stepping to the horses, he gathered up reins to lead part of them away. Vince went to the ravines, where Arabella and her father were standing at the edge, watching with anticipation as the soldiers moved stones and prowled about in the brush. Climbing down into a ravine, Vince helped two men move a huge rock and then joined the soldiers in their search.

A few soldiers found pieces of wood, raising outcries and creating moments of excitement, but all of the uncovered treasure turned out to be weathered trunks of mesquite trees that had fallen into the ravine.

Once the tent was set up, Arabella occasionally persuaded her father to sit in it out of the wind and sun, but he always returned after a few minutes. At midday, there was a break for lunch, and then the search resumed. The drivers and servants had grown tired of sitting around at the camp by then and trekked up to join the soldiers after the meal.

While going from one ravine to another during the afternoon, Vince glimpsed someone on the western side of the mesa at the ruins. He rushed up the slope and stepped into his saddle, riding across the mesa and down through the brush in time to confront Murillo as he was leaving the ruins.

"I told everyone to stay away from here," Vince said curtly as he reined his horse.

The man's coarse features flushed with anger, and then he grimaced, his hand reaching down to the leg that had been injured during the thunderstorm. "I merely went close enough to look," he said with a shrug.

Glancing at the ruins, Vince saw that Murillo's footprints covered the entire area. The man's shoes had square toes and elevated heels, and it was obvious that the prints were his. "From now on, you stay completely away from those ruins," Vince said, then turned his horse.

Only when Vince was sure the man was going for a horse to return to camp did he rejoin the others. An hour later, the sun sinking deep in the west, Vince sent a soldier to get horses for everyone except the lookouts to ride back to camp.

The following morning, when everyone went back to the top of the mesa and the search resumed, Vince tried to think of methods that might be more rewarding than rummaging about in the ravines. One that occurred to him immediately was to take a closer look at the far end of the ravines, where he had warned the soldiers not to go. He decided to go to the foot of the mesa and look up at the ends of the ravines through his binoculars.

He rode back off the mesa and around to the northern side, then examined the debris at the end of the ravines. Thick pieces of wood jutted up among it, but as he peered more closely through his binoculars, the pieces all appeared to be trunks of fallen trees. Slowly he moved along the foot of the mesa, reining up every few steps to search the ravines.

The rock face was mottled with shades of gray and black, making any irregularities difficult to see. As a result, Vince almost missed the opening of a cave as he scanned the binoculars from one ravine to another.

Moving the binoculars back, he was still uncertain that the irregular black shape a few yards below the top of the cliff was the mouth of a cave.

Riding a few paces, he checked again from a different angle. Indeed, it was a cave. It satisfied the priest's description as a comfortable place during severe weather, and it looked out toward the north. In addition, a faint line in the stone reached from the cave up to the edge of the mesa, possibly where a narrow path had been carved and since had eroded and fallen away. Vince turned his horse, touching it with his spurs.

As he raced to the top of the mesa, he realized that he could raise false hopes that could end in severe disappointment, and he reined his horse to a slow canter. The search had moved down toward the west corner of the mesa, while the cave was near the northeast corner. Riding toward the edge above it, he beckoned Sergeant Henshaw.

Mounting up, the sergeant rode over to Vince. "I want to take a look over the edge there," Vince casually said. "I'll use the rope on my saddle, and I'll need a couple of men to make sure the end stays firm."

The sergeant saluted, riding away as Vince dismounted. Looking around, he found a thick length of mesquite and dragged it to the edge to keep the rope from fraying against the rock. Then he tied one end of the rope around a boulder. Henshaw returned with two soldiers, who checked the knot at the boulder as the sergeant steadied the rope across the mesquite.

Slowly Vince climbed over the edge, gripped the rope between his feet, and slid down. When the cave came into view, he swung himself toward it, stepping onto a narrow ledge in front of it. He had to stoop low to enter the opening, which let out into a roomy chamber. Unable to see anything in the dim light, he struck a match, and the flickering light shone on dusty earthenware vessels, leather bags, and baskets. Lifting the match higher, he saw a skeleton at one side of the cave.

He moved toward it, stepping through the undisturbed dust of centuries.

The rib bones were broken, and an arrowhead lay among them, revealing the cause of death. Seeing a large silver cross among the bones, Vince dropped the spent match and struck another one, bending low to make out the cursive engraving. After polishing it with his shirtsleeve, he saw it was a name, that of Eusebio Armero y Carranza. His heart quickened, and he felt a thrill of anticipation, eager to share the news with Arabella and her father.

Two skeletons lay on the other side of the cave, with simple wooden crosses lying among their bones. Carved on the crosses were the names of Luiz Obregon and José Toral. One skeleton had an arrowhead embedded in a thigh bone; the other, an arrowhead among broken shoulder bones. Vince stepped carefully to the side of the skeletons, where some earthenware vessels and baskets lay. He struck another match and saw that they contained dust, possibly the remains of food. The leather bags were there, too, and he lifted the flaps on them to peer inside. There were the mission valuables, and he was surprised to see that they appeared to fulfill the most extravagant legends about the treasure.

Stepping back to the mouth of the cave, Vince stood still for several minutes. He was gripped by a sense of wonder over what he had found. In a sense he had reached two centuries into the past and unraveled a mystery.

From above, the sergeant called out in a worried voice. "Have you found something down there to stand on, Captain Bolton? Are you all right?"

"Yes, I'm coming back up now," Vince replied.

He gripped the rope firmly, clamping the rope between his feet, and climbed up it. When he reached the top, Sergeant Henshaw gave him his hand, and Vince made his way over the edge just as Arabella and her father arrived.

"I saw a cave a few yards below the edge of the mesa

and climbed down to look in it," he told them. "Padre Eusebio's remains are in the cave."

Arabella's eyes opened wide with shock, and then a radiant smile of delight wreathed her features as she turned to her father. Don Raimundo remained solemn, as if fearing that Vince had made a mistake. "Are you sure what you saw is Padre Eusebio's remains, Captain?" he asked. "Are you certain of what you say?"

"I'm absolutely positive, Don Raimundo. A cross with the remains is engraved with Padre Eusebio's name."

Henshaw spread the news to the rest of the party, shouting, "The captain has found the priest's bones! Captain Bolton did it!" Cupping his hands around his mouth, he bellowed at the men still searching the ravines along the edge of the mesa. "You men get on up here! Captain Bolton has found the priest's bones!"

His voice was almost drowned by the triumphant whoops of the others. Finally Don Raimundo smiled, and he and Arabella hugged each other in joy.

Then the grandee grasped Vince's arm urgently. "I must go down to the cave myself to see Padre Eusebio's remains and the other things, just as they are, Captain."

"No," Vince replied firmly. "That's completely out of the question. It would be impossible for you to climb down a rope and then climb back up, and it would be virtually as dangerous for you to be lowered on a rope and pulled back up. You can't go to the cave, Don Raimundo."

"Please, Captain, please," the aged man insisted. "This is something I must do, and you are a man who finds ways for things to be done. Please, find a way for me to do this."

His voice was urgent, and Vince hesitated. The grandee's tone also seemed to change Arabella's mind, erasing her frown of disapproval over what he wanted to do. She looked up at Vince, her large, beautiful eyes pleading, and then he knew he had to find a way.

It took an hour to have a sling made in which to lower the grandee and to have the rosewood coffin unpacked from the wagons and brought with other supplies to the edge of the ravine. But then, with the soldiers' help, Vince lowered Don Raimundo down to the cave in the canvas sling, followed by Arabella. After Vince descended to the cave, the rosewood coffin and two boxes were lowered.

"Padre Eusebio and the two friars apparently died of wounds," Vince explained, once they were inside the cave. "It was probably not long after they arrived here. It's a miracle they even reached it, wounded and loaded down with all they were carrying."

Vince lit a lantern that had been lowered, and the grandee took out his rosary. Arabella also took out her rosary as she stepped to her father's side, and the two knelt beside the priest's remains. For a moment they prayed silently, and then she helped her father up and they began putting the remains into the boxes.

Several minutes later, Arabella sat in the sling again as the soldiers pulled her up. Don Raimundo was hoisted back up next, and then Vince tied the boxes to the sling for them to be hauled up. The sling was lowered again, and this time he sent up everything else salvaged from the cave. The costly gold artifacts in the leather bags were last. Then Vince climbed back up.

Once on the mesa, the treasure was laid out on the ground, a dazzling array in the sunlight. The centerpiece was a large crucifix that was some fifteen pounds of solid gold. Smaller crosses weighing about five pounds each were adorned with diamonds and rubies, the metal gleaming and the gems sparkling in the light, and a pair of large, ornate chalices were also set with precious stones. In addition, there were salvers, incense burners, and candlesticks made of solid gold.

Vince ended the moment of silent awe among the people by turning to the sergeant and giving him orders to prepare to leave. He wanted to cover a few miles before nightfall rather than run the risk of having the Indians find them near the sacred ground. And now that the treasure had been secured, it was time to put into action the plan he and Don Raimundo had devised to trap the man who had tried to assassinate the grandee.

Chapter Eleven

Vince Bolton called for the long column of travelers to halt early that night, since the day's events had exhausted the party. Everyone retired for the night as soon as dinner was finished, and soon they were all asleep. No one was awake to observe a man push aside his blankets and creep toward Don Raimundo's wagon.

The man was guided to the grandee by a lantern shining dimly through the canvas that covered the wagon bed. Silently the man climbed into it and smiled grimly with satisfaction as he looked at the still form in the blankets. Taking out his knife, he knelt beside the bed. The bag containing the treasure from the mesa was at the end of the wagon, and he glanced at it as he lifted the knife.

Suddenly a hand shot out from the blankets and seized the man's wrist. It was a brawny hand, gripping the arm tightly. Then the blankets were tossed aside, revealing Vince Bolton, who sat up quickly on the bed. "I thought all along that it was you, Murillo," he growled.

An involuntary squeal of shock and terror burst from Federico Murillo's throat as he tried to pull away. But Vince's fingers were like a steel vise, tightening with a crushing pressure, and soon Murillo's hand went numb. The knife dropped to the bed, making no noise as it fell into the blankets. In the next instant Vince Bolton threw him down on the wagon's floor and searched him.

The captain found Murillo's pistol, tossed it aside, and then dragged him toward the end of the wagon.

Panic gripped Murillo. Instead of the wealth he had envisioned, he was faced with prison. He tried again to get away from Bolton, but the tall, muscular man who was effortlessly hauling him out of the wagon appeared not even to notice.

Murillo reached to his lapel, where one weapon that the captain had failed to detect still remained hidden. Then he stopped himself. The knife under his lapel was as sharp as a scalpel but no larger than a hatpin. With an expert thrust to a vulnerable spot, it would kill even the captain, but the chances of being able to do that in his present situation were poor. Logic dictated that he wait; perhaps he would use it to cut his bonds and flee.

"The plan worked, Don Raimundo," Bolton called out, guiding the limping man across the camp. "It was Murillo, and I caught him in the act."

"You weren't injured in any way, were you?" Don Raimundo asked.

"No, he didn't injure me," the captain answered, shoving Murillo toward the fire. Murillo almost stumbled and fell into it.

The fire blazed up as the grandee tossed wood onto it. "Well, well, Señor Murillo, what am I to do with you?" the elderly man mused. Then he turned to the captain. "May I offer him his freedom in exchange for information about those who hired him as an assassin, Captain?"

"I'm sorry, but no," Bolton replied firmly. "He committed the crime of attempted murder in a territory of the United States. Legally I'm bound to turn him over to the authorities for trial."

"I was sure that would be your reaction," Don Raimundo commented, shrugging whimsically. "Very well, Señor Murillo, I have nothing to offer you. On the other hand, you have nothing to offer me that I will not find out in due course after I return to Spain."

The servants and several of the soldiers were looking at Murillo with curiosity as they moved closer to the fire. Then Arabella emerged from her tent. Wrapping her robe around herself, she stepped toward the fire and asked her father what had happened. After the grandee briefly explained, the dark-eyed woman stiffened with rage and turned on Murillo, verbally castigating him.

As she moved toward him, shouting angrily, Murillo saw a possible way out of his situation, one that would still provide him with great wealth. Arabella was still too far away but was moving closer, and he poised himself, ready to reach for the knife under his lapel.

"Why did you do it?" she demanded. "Why would you do such a thing?"

Murillo searched for a reply that would provoke her further and then answered coldly, "For money, of course."

Her eyes snapped with anger as she took a long step closer and berated him. The captain, frowning, was just telling her to move back when Murillo leapt toward her and seized her, plucking out the knife. The captain's right hand was a blur, lifting the flap on his holster, but Murillo quickly put the knife to Arabella's throat. "Don't!" he shouted. "I will kill her!"

Bolton froze, his revolver halfway out of the holster. He was an image of frustrated rage as he glanced at Murillo.

Now that the tables had turned, Murillo felt flush with confidence, and he laughed gleefully as he looked at the grandee. "I believe I now have something to offer you, Don Raimundo," he jeered. "Your daughter's life, no less."

"What do you want, Murillo?" Don Raimundo asked quietly.

"Two horses, one saddled. On the other one I want my belongings, an ample supply of food and water, and the Gran Quivira treasure."

The grandee nodded calmly. "Very well. Now release Señorita Arabella."

"First I must have your absolute assurance that you will fulfill your side of the bargain, Don Raimundo."

"I give you my absolute assurance that I will do as I said. Now release the señorita immediately."

Knowing that the grandee was a man of the highest integrity whose word could be trusted implicitly, Murillo turned her loose.

As Arabella ran to her father, the captain charged toward Murillo and pulled out his pistol, snarling, "I didn't promise you anything, Murillo!"

"Please, Captain!" Don Raimundo shouted. "I gave him my assurance, and I beg you to honor it!"

Bolton was already in front of Murillo, his pistol at arm's length and the hammer thumbed back. Murillo quailed in stark, icy fear.

"Please, Captain!" Don Raimundo repeated. "I gave him my assurance, and if you kill him it will be a dishonor upon me!"

For a second, which seemed like an eternity to Murillo, he knew his life hung by a bare, thin thread. Then the captain eased the hammer down, jammed the revolver into his holster, and turned away.

"Sergeant Henshaw!" Bolton barked over his shoulder.

"Yes, sir?" the sergeant replied.

"Put Murillo's belongings on a packhorse along with a supply of food and water and the bag containing the gold articles. And have a horse saddled for him to ride."

The sergeant, pointing to the men, relayed the orders, and they began to scurry about. One tied up Murillo's bedroll, and others ran to get the horses and other things. Everyone else stood in silence and waited, except Vince Bolton. He was so furious that he was unable to be still. The muscles in the sides of his face worked as he paced impatiently, his brows furrowed.

Finally Murillo saw the soldiers leading the horses to him. He took the reins of the saddle horse, and as he started to mount, a large hand gripped his shoulder with crushing force and spun him around. It was Captain Bolton. Before Murillo could react, the captain had gripped the front of his coat, lifting him off his feet.

"You're a dead man, Murillo," Bolton said quietly, their noses an inch apart. "The world isn't big enough for you to hide from me. Even if it takes the rest of my life, I'll see you dead. Now get out of here!"

He flung Murillo against the horse and then turned and stamped away. Murillo caught the stirrup to keep from sprawling and, regaining his balance, mounted the horse. With the packhorse following, he rode toward the edge of the camp.

The captain's threat still rang in Murillo's ears as he rode southward through the darkness. Then he managed to force it to the back of his mind, thinking of the turn of events.

He had burned with envy for those like the Carranzas, wealthy people who took luxuries for granted. Just before he left Spain, he was offered a way to obtain a substantial fortune. In addition to the money, it provided a means for him to vent his hatred on at least one member of the wealthy and powerful class. All he had to do was see that Don Raimundo did not return to Spain alive.

The first opportunity to kill the grandee came after the departure from Socorro, when he had poisoned the laudanum. Far from any doctor who might identify the cause of death, the others in the party—Murillo had reasoned—would consider the death simply unfortunate, the result of an aged man's taking laudanum while on an arduous journey. As long as he disposed of the laudanum before returning to the town, so no one could have it analyzed, there was no way that Don Raimundo's death could possibly be pinned on him. That plan had collapsed, however, when the poisoned laudanum was administered to the boy and it was necessary for him to get rid of the rest of it quickly. And the attempt to kill Don Raimundo with the rattlesnake had also proved unsuccessful, as had his attempt to use the dagger on the old man during the thunderstorm.

Murillo had been disgusted and disappointed when those plans failed, but he was now delighted beyond description by the present turn of events. He would be unable to collect the reward that had been promised to him in Spain for killing Don Raimundo, of course, but that amount was modest compared to the value of the gold. It would provide luxuries for the rest of his life.

Reining up, he opened the bag on the packhorse and took out one of the chalices. After fastening the bag securely, he rode on, feeling the heavy weight of the gold goblet and fondling the gems on it. Any one of the gems was worth far more than Murillo had earned in years, and he chuckled gleefully as he caressed the jewel-encrusted gold. Life was beginning to feel sweet for the first time, he thought.

Waking slowly two mornings later, Federico Murillo opened his eyes and then sat up in shock. At first he felt as though he were dreaming. He had heard nothing, which seemed impossible and made him doubt the evidence of his senses. Then, icy fear gripping him, he knew that what he was seeing was all too real.

Some two score Indians were sitting and standing about in the sandy arroyo where he had stopped the night before to camp. A few more were with the horses at the edge of the arroyo, while a tall, lean half-breed sat beside the fire, close enough to touch Murillo. Wrapped in ragged robes and holding weapons, some with feathers in bands around their shaggy hair, all the Indians were silent and motionless as they stared at Murillo, their bronze features stolid, their dark eyes menacing.

Looking around in fright, Murillo wondered how long they had been there, watching him sleep. One was much older than the others, with deep lines and wrinkles in his leathery face, and he sat by himself a few feet away. He murmured something in his language to the half-breed and then pointed toward Murillo.

"I am called Dark Cloud," the half-breed said in heavily accented Mexican Spanish. "Do you understand what I say?"

"Yes, yes," Murillo stuttered. "What do you want?"

Making no reply, the half-breed picked up a long, thin twig beside the fire and placed the tip of it in the embers. As it began to smolder, a wisp of smoke rose from it, and Dark Cloud picked up a larger stick, which he used to push the blanket away from Murillo's bare feet. Shivering with terror, Murillo drew his feet closer to his body, and Dark Cloud pushed more of the blanket aside. Murillo pulled his feet higher, and Dark Cloud uncovered them again. Finally, when Murillo could get his feet no higher, the half-breed pointed toward Murillo's horses. "Those horses belonged to Mescalero warriors. Where did you get them?"

Anticipating the need to lie, Murillo kept his reply brief in order to preserve possibilities for elaboration later. "I got them from soldiers who said they captured them from Indians."

"You were traveling with the soldiers? Why did you leave them?"

"We argued, and I went my own way."

The half-breed asked other questions about the soldiers, including their number, what direction they were traveling in, and their present location. Occasionally the older Indian interjected questions in Apache, and Dark Cloud translated. The aged man clearly understood the replies in Spanish, and that led Murillo to believe that he considered it beneath him to address the Spaniard directly.

Murillo hoped that the Indians merely wanted to know about the troop and would ride away when their curiosity was satisfied. But the half-breed's attitude remained threatening in a cold, detached way as he reached over now and then with the stick to keep the blanket pushed away from Murillo's feet.

Then the half-breed pointed the stick toward Murillo's belongings, and spoke to a warrior in Apache. Stepping forward, the warrior opened the bags and dumped them. When he opened the bag containing the treasures, a chorus of guttural exclamations of surprise and keen interest rose among the Indians.

It immediately subsided when the older Indian pointed to the gold objects and spoke quietly to Dark Cloud. The half-breed turned back to Murillo. "Where did you get those?" he asked.

"I took them from the soldiers."

The older Indian muttered another question, which the half-breed repeated in Spanish. "What is the leader of the soldiers called?"

"Bolton. Captain Vincent Bolton."

When the older Indian murmured a phrase, Dark Cloud picked up the twig from the fire, its tip by now a fiery ember. "Do not move," he warned. "If you move, I will have you staked to the ground. Chief White Eagle says that you speak with a forked tongue. You lie, because one like you could not take anything from the soldier named Bolton. You must feel pain so you will speak the truth, but if you move, you will have much greater pain."

As the glowing ember slowly traced a searing path across the instep of Murillo's foot, his strong, instinctive reaction was to jerk away from it, and he struggled desperately against it, the dire threat about moving still ringing in his ears. Staying motionless seemed to make the pain much worse, and a whimper rose in his throat and turned into a shrill scream of agony. Then he began babbling an explanation.

"There is a woman with the soldiers," he stammered. "I captured her and threatened to kill her unless I got what I wanted, and they gave me what I asked. They gave me horses, food, and water, and the gold."

The explanation satisfied the chief, who muttered another question, which Dark Cloud translated. "Where did the soldiers get the gold?"

"Chupadera Mesa."

A stir passed through the Indians, and Murillo knew he had said the wrong thing. White Eagle's wrinkled face remained impassive, but somehow it reflected sudden rage. "*I* did not go on the mesa," Murillo added quickly. "I heard that it is sacred, so I stayed away when the others went up to—"

He broke off when the chief gestured impatiently. Then Dark Cloud turned to Murillo and lifted a fist in fury. White Eagle stood up and beckoned the Indians on the edge of the arroyo who were with the horses. The horses were herded down into the arroyo, and Dark Cloud snapped orders. One Indian hastily stuffed the gold articles back into the bag and tied it while others gathered up their weapons and mounted. Murillo's belongings were left scattered on the ground, and he barely had time to dress before he was shoved onto one of the horses.

As they rode away from the arroyo, White Eagle led them to the northeast, toward Chupadera Mesa. Riding near Dark Cloud, Murillo tried to talk, wanting to get some idea of what might happen to him, but the half-breed ignored him.

Since his saddle had been left behind, Murillo rode bareback like the Indians. For the first hour he gripped the horse with his legs to keep from bouncing, but then the muscles in his legs gave out. After that, with every stride the horse took, he felt as though he were falling two feet onto a hard surface, the shock snapping his back and passing up through his body.

As the hours wore on, the lingering pain in his blistered foot was nothing compared to the pain throughout his body. The suffocating heat of the day settled, and each gasping breath he took burned in his lungs. He was hungry and thirsty, while every muscle in his body ached from the relentless pounding as he clutched the horse's mane and bounced limply on its back.

The lean, wiry Indians rode like machines, tirelessly and effortlessly, as they kept up the hard, driving gait. When the torrid heat of the afternoon came, the sun glared down from the cloudless sky, further depleting him of energy and moisture, but the Indians continued their relentless pace. Dazed with pain and fatigue, Murillo numbly held onto the horse, fearing sudden death if he caused the Indians any inconvenience.

The trek finally ended late in the day at the head of a valley, where scraggly vegetation grew around a tiny spring. When Murillo fell off his horse and was unable to move, the Indians chuckled with grim amusement. They drank from the spring and filled large containers made of skins. Parched with thirst, Murillo finally summoned the strength to crawl to the spring and gulp down the tepid, brackish water. Afterward, he immediately sank into the deep slumber of exhaustion.

It seemed only moments later that a moccasined foot stirred him roughly, awakening him. The night had passed already, and the Indians were mounting up before the sun rose. Struggling to his feet, he went to his horse, his body wracked with pain.

Murillo sank into a haze of suffering during that day. The hard ride across the arid hills and arroyos became a grueling nightmare that was punctuated with brief moments of respite. As long as the ride continued, he knew he would at least be allowed to live, but at length that became less important to him. More than anything else, he yearned for this torture to end, regardless of what awaited him when it was finished.

It ended during the sultry hours of the afternoon, when the mesa emerged from the blur of heat waves ahead. Upon reaching it, all of the Indians except for the chief made camp, while the aged man went up onto the mesa. Several hours later, as the sun was setting, he returned. His face was expressionless, but a seething rage was evident in his dark, glittering eyes.

He spoke tersely to Dark Cloud, who turned to Murillo. "You did not go onto the mesa?" the half-breed asked.

"No, I did not. The others did, but I heard that it is sacred to Indians, so I stayed away."

His eyes smoldering, the chief waited until Murillo had finished. Then he pointed to Murillo's shoes. With a sinking sensation in the pit of his stomach, Murillo remembered the footprints he had left around the ruins on the mesa.

Icy terror gripping him, Murillo also thought about what happened the last time White Eagle was dissatisfied with what he had said. He was not eager to feel his skin burn again.

The chief snapped an order, gesturing to the Indians. Several of them seized Murillo, dragged him to his horse, and pushed him onto it. Leading his horse, they followed Dark Cloud and White Eagle, heading around the southern end of the mesa and up to the top of it.

At the mesa's peak, they crossed to the ruins, then dismounted and pulled Murillo from his horse. While four of the Indians started to dig a hole in front of the ruins, White Eagle chanted, the rhythm growing more frenzied as the hole got deeper.

"What is the chief doing?" Murillo asked Dark Cloud.

"He is appeasing the sacred spirits of the mesa," the Indian replied with a tone of derision.

Cold sweat streamed down Murillo's face as he watched the hole grow larger and larger, fearful of what was to be placed in it. When at last the hole was deep enough, the Indians dragged him forward. The chief pointed, murmuring an order, and the Indians jerked Murillo's shoes off his feet and handed them to White Eagle. Turning toward the ruins, the chief held the shoes over his head and chanted for a moment, and then he threw the shoes into the hole.

The Indian with the bag of stolen gold artifacts stepped forward, handing it to the chief. White Eagle lifted it over his head, chanted again, and then upended it, dumping the shining treasures into the hole. As the chief again chanted, the Indians holding Murillo lifted him bodily and carried his struggling form toward the hole. Thrashing about, he screamed shrilly, but his effort was in vain. They dropped him into the hole.

The impact momentarily stunned Murillo as he landed on his head and shoulders at the bottom of the pit. When several Indians began pouring dirt and rock on him, panic seized him. He scrambled frantically, trying to turn around to climb out of the hole, but the Indians beat him back. Soon the weight pressing down on him was heavy, and he could not move.

With the dirt closing off all sounds from above, the only thing Murillo could hear was his hoarse gasping for breath as his lungs burned and labored. He felt the gold under his hand and grasped one of the treasures tightly as he prepared to die.

Riding at the head of the column, Vince Bolton glanced back at the stagecoach and wagons moving smoothly uphill behind him. The horses were maintaining a fast walk as they followed the tracks that had been made on the eastward journey. They were covering the distance much more rapidly than they had when they were heading toward Gran Quivira.

Arabella, riding beside the captain, pointed to the west, where the mountains towered high and dark above the haze of heat waves. "We can see the mountains clearly now, even during the hottest part of the day," she remarked.

"Yes," Vince replied. "If we keep up this pace, we should reach the foothills in about two days."

She smiled at him through the veil protecting her face from the sun, and then she looked ahead again. Vince's eyes lingered on her. Even obscured by the voile draped down from her wide hat, her face was rapturously lovely.

When a roar of gunfire came from an arroyo seventy-five yards away on the column's left flank and bullets slammed into the vehicles, the horses reared in fright. Vince reacted instantly. Leaning over, he put an arm around Arabella's waist, lifted her off her horse, and put her on the ground. "Get in the coach with your father, and both of you get on the floor!" he said. "Run, Arabella. *Run!*"

As she lifted her hem and darted toward the coach,

Vince wheeled his horse around and shouted for the
troops to fire at will. Aiming, he assessed the change in
the gunfire from the gully after the first volley and
knew the enemy was not disciplined—and not accustomed to facing gunfire.

As the troops fired their carbines, bullets whistled,
and dust erupted around the weapons from enemy gunfire. A bullet traced a fiery path on the left side of
Vince's chest, grazing his ribs. From the corner of his
eye he saw a soldier reel in the saddle as a bullet struck
him; then the man straightened back up. "Forward at a
gallop, ho!" Vince shouted. "Increase fire to rapid fire!"

The horses surged into a gallop, and the gunfire became a battering roar on each side of Vince as the men
worked the levers on their carbines and squeezed off
shots. The steady volleys from the troops' firearms were
causing most of the gunmen in the arroyo to keep their
heads down, and only occasionally did one of them fire a
shot.

Fifty yards from the gully, the reports from the carbines began to fade, and then the hammer on Vince's
carbine fell on an empty chamber. Pushing the carbine
into the saddle scabbard, he took out his pistol. "Rapid
fire with pistols!" he shouted. "Fire at will!"

The gunfire from the arroyo increased while the carbines were hastily being jammed into their scabbards
and revolvers were drawn. But it died away once more
when the soldiers' gunfire resumed. As the distance to
the arroyo closed, Vince saw movements through the
dust hanging over the gully as some of the attackers
raised their heads to fire. Thumbing the hammer back
on his pistol, he quickly took aim and snapped off shots
at them.

Pistol bullets ricocheted down into the arroyo at the
closer range, and the horses tethered in it suddenly
flooded out the opposite side, breaking their picket
rope in panic. Five men raced after the horses, trying to
mount up and flee. Getting his first good look at the

attackers, Vince saw that they were common outlaws
wearing disheveled, ragged clothing.

The five were also the first good targets, in full view of
the troop. They staggered and fell as the pistols roared,
and the horses scattered across the field beyond the
gully. At twenty-five yards from the arroyo, Vince fired
the last shot in his pistol and holstered it. Spurring his
horse, he drew his saber. "Sabers!" he shouted.
"Charge, *now*!"

The men drew their sabers and, leaning low in the
saddle and spurring their horses into a headlong run,
pointed them forward. As the troop swept ahead in a
thunder of pounding hoofbeats, only scattered shots
came from the arroyo. Vince saw one man's mouth drop
open in consternation as he looked at the line of bright
steel blades bearing down; then the man ducked out of
sight.

Charging over the edge, Vince's horse plunged down
the steep slope. Two men rolled under its hooves as it
slid and scrambled for footing. He stabbed at one, and
the blade sank into the man's chest. Jerking it free, he
slashed at the other one, cutting him down.

The center of the arroyo turned into a wild pandemonium of hand-to-hand battle, a packed mass of plunging
horses and men locked in mortal struggle. In the midst
of the melee, Vince's horse stumbled and went down on
its belly, and a man directly in front of it lifted his pistol
toward the captain. Vince whipped his saber around,
and the man's mouth opened wide in a scream that was
lost in the bedlam as his pistol flew through the air. He
fell as Vince stabbed him in the chest.

Vince pulled his horse to its feet with the reins, re-
mounted, and spurred toward a man who was trying to
climb out of the arroyo. The captain's horse almost fell,
stumbling over bodies as it raced toward the man, but
Vince managed to keep it afoot. Upon reaching the
fleeing outlaw, Vince slashed his blade across the man's
legs, and he rolled down the slope, trying to lift a pistol.
Leaning low in the saddle, Vince spurred his horse to-

vard the man and stabbed him; then he pulled the
blade free and glanced around for another foe.

The battle had become a rout and was starting to turn
into a slaughter. The arroyo was littered with bodies,
and the rest of the attackers were trying to flee. The
soldiers, their gleaming blades red with blood as they
lashed right and left, chased after the men. Vince
leaned down, wiped his saber on a body, and then
sheathed it. Taking out his pistol, he dumped the empty
shells from the cylinder and quickly reloaded it.

"Take prisoners if they offer to surrender, troopers!"
he shouted. "Don't kill any who want to surrender!"

The sergeant took up the cry, bellowing at the men.
As the battle faded away into an uneasy, dangerous
aftermath, Vince cocked his pistol and glanced in both
directions along the arroyo. Seeing an outlaw lifting a
rifle, he took quick aim and fired. The man sprawled, a
bullet through his head.

"Troopers, chop off any head that doesn't immediately have two hands on top of it!" Vince shouted.

The soldiers lifted their sabers menacingly, and the
outlaws quickly put their hands on their heads. Vince
counted eight of them. Getting a closer look, he recognized a couple of them from the Sundowner Saloon,
and instantly he knew who had been behind the attack.
He also knew that Big Jim Congor would be far from
danger, hiding in a safe place.

"All right, disarm them and get them out of here.
We'll take them back as prisoners," he ordered. "Sergeant Henshaw, check the troop and take a casualty
count."

Vince rode out of the arroyo, seething with anger. He
wanted to go after Congor immediately, but other
things came first. As he cantered toward the stagecoach
to check on Arabella and her father, he saw them step
down from the coach, neither of them harmed, and felt
a great sense of relief. Reining up, he said, "I'm glad you
weren't hurt."

Arabella looked up at his tunic with alarm. "There is

blood on your coat, Vincent!" she exclaimed. "You have
been wounded!"

"It's only a scratch. The sergeant is checking the men,
and I'd appreciate it if you would have the servants see
to any who are wounded."

"I will take care of them myself," she said, "and the
servants will assist me. Come with me, Vincent, and I
will attend to your wound first."

"No, no. It's very minor, and others are in much more
need of your attention. Besides, there are things I must
do now." He lifted a hand, shaking his head as she
started to protest. "I'll be back presently and have it
seen to, but there are things I must do that cannot wait.
If you'll see to the wounded men, I'll be very grateful."

Arabella nodded reluctantly as Vince reined his horse
around and rode back to the arroyo, where the prisoners were being guarded by two soldiers. Several of the
soldiers were sitting on the ground, blood on their tu-
nics and faces, and the sergeant was examining them.

Henshaw turned as Vince rode up. "Captain, we've
got eight men with flesh wounds. Two more men are
unfit for duty, each of them with a bullet in his shoulder.
And one more has a bad cut on his head. A few of the
horses have scrapes and flesh wounds, but nothing serious. Twenty-two enemy dead, sir."

"Send the wounded over to the wagons, where they
will be taken care of. Then send some men to round up
those loose horses over there." At Vince's orders, the
soldiers herded the outlaws away. "You," Vince said,
pointing to one of them, "where is Congor?"

"He's up there somewhere," the man muttered, gesturing toward the foothills.

Vince turned to Henshaw. "I'm going after him, Sergeant. Take command here and make camp. I'll be back
after I've dealt with Congor."

"All right, sir. But if he's up in the foothills, he might
be hard to find. Aren't you going to take some men with
you?"

Vince was reloading his pistol, and he shook his head.

"No." He took out his carbine to reload it, adding, "Congor is a man who likes his comforts. I'll start looking for him at the Carlson ranch and track him down from there."

Peering through binoculars from a bluff in the foothills, Big Jim Congor felt numb. Sitting on his horse, he had been watching the scene intently for several minutes, and now he was frozen with disbelief. Lew Frable, beside Congor, cleared his throat nervously and said, "We'd better get out of here, Big Jim."

Lowering the binoculars, Congor stared blankly into space, stupefied. While watching the brief, savage battle, he had experienced shock, rage, and a range of other emotions. Now he felt drained, overcome by the enormity of his misjudgment. Feeling totally confident of victory before the battle, he was stunned now by the utterly disastrous defeat.

Congor nodded absently in agreement. "Yes, let's go to the ranch for supplies. Then we'll make a run for it."

As they made their way to the road and then turned toward the Carlson ranch, Congor thought about Vince Bolton and all that he had done against Congor before. Suddenly it occurred to him that it would be uncharacteristic of Bolton to send a column of soldiers chasing after him; after all, Bolton was the man who had marched into the saloon alone with the infuriating confidence that he could deal with anything that happened. No, Congor reflected, the captain would come by himself.

Congor realized that Bolton's stubborn insistence on chasing him down alone would present a perfect opportunity for revenge, and by a relatively simple means: a shot from a rifle in ambush. Having just watched the result of one cataclysmic misjudgment, Congor thought about the idea carefully, wondering if he might be underestimating Bolton again. Then, smiling to himself, he shrugged off that worry. Bolton was a formidable enemy, but he was not superhuman. A rifle bullet would kill him just as quickly as it would anyone else.

Frable looked down at Congor's horse and frowned. With each stride it was making a metallic clanking noise with its rear hoof. "It sounds like one of that horse's shoes is comin' loose, Big Jim," he said, "and these are the only two horses we have left. I don't know nothin' about fixin' a horse's shoes. Do you?"

Congor shrugged indifferently and looked thoughtfully at Frable. His plans had no place for the man, who had served his purpose and was nothing more than a hindrance to him. And nothing was wrong with the horse *he* was riding, Congor thought. "No, but it doesn't make any difference."

"But if the horse loses that shoe, Big Jim, it won't get very far before it goes lame."

"It'll get far enough."

Glancing at the horse's rear hooves again, Frable nodded uncertainly as Congor and he turned off the road at the ranch. They passed the springhouse and the charred timbers of the house, reining up at the barn. Once they had gone inside, Frable took a gunnysack and hastily filled it with some canned goods they had found there. Congor picked up a rifle, looked it over carefully, and checked the magazine.

Frable took a last look around, then tied the top of the bag. "Well, this will last us a good while, Big Jim," he said. "I'll carry it on my horse so yours won't have any extra weight on that loose shoe."

"Very well," Congor replied, his back to Frable. Tucking the rifle under his arm, he took out his derringer and cocked both hammers. Then he turned, holding it at arm's length.

In the next instant Congor aimed the pistol six inches from Frable's forehead and pulled both triggers. Astonishment and fear were just starting to spread over Frable's face when the bullets ripped into his head. Dropping the bag, he staggered backward and fell.

Congor methodically reloaded the derringer and put it
away, then carried the bag and rifle outside.

He tied the bag on the horse Frable had been riding
and then clambered heavily onto the saddle. As he
turned toward the road, he checked the rifle again,
smiling grimly to himself. He knew Vince Bolton would
be coming for him—and this time he would be ready.

Passing through the first upswell of foothills, Vince
saw innumerable hoofprints made in the recent past
and guessed that they must be the trails left by lookouts
Congor had posted. Radiating in a fan into the flatlands,
they came together at the beginning of the narrow road
that led past the Carlson ranch and up through the
mountains. Nothing disturbed the quiet as he went up
the road, turning off at the ranch.

Seeing a horse tethered in front of the barn, Vince
reined up at the springhouse and dismounted. He took
out his pistol and walked slowly toward the barn. The
hinges on the wide front door squeaked as he nudged it
open and held the pistol ready to fire. He stepped inside, looked at the body, and glanced around at the
litter of food cases and other things. After seeing all he
needed to, he left the barn and returned to his horse.

West of the ranch, Vince held his horse back to a walk
and studied the hoofprints on the road. The column on
its eastward journey had left a mass of tracks, overlaid
with others left by Congor and his men. In the muddle
of hoof marks, Vince picked out a fresh set made by a
horse going westward up the road.

His carbine resting across the saddle, Vince followed
the trail up the road. A short time later he heard a jay
squawking noisily around a curve ahead, and he reined
up and listened. Knowing that the jay could be signaling
a disturbance—which might be Congor—he decided to
take no chances. Dismounting, he tethered his horse.

Cutting quietly through the forest, Vince came
through the trees beyond the curved part of the road.
He glimpsed a horse and then took a few more steps

and saw Congor. The fat man was sitting behind a boulder with a rifle resting across it; he was thumbing through a notebook.

"Put up your hands, Congor!" Vince called.

Startled by the shout, Congor dropped the notebook as his bulging body jerked and he grabbed for the rifle.

"Don't try it, Congor!" Vince warned him. "You don't have a chance!"

The man's sagging face swiveled around as his hand poised over the rifle. His beady eyes glaring, he hesitated, though he trembled with fury. Then he snatched up the rifle and threw himself to one side as he swung the weapon around.

Vince, having anticipated the movement, tracked Congor in the sights of the carbine and squeezed the trigger. The left side of the big man's coat flapped as the bullet thudded into him, and the impact of the slug threw him back against the boulder, his eyes opening wide with shock and disbelief. He screamed shrilly in terror, as though realizing that his life was draining away, and then he slumped.

Vince brought Congor's horse closer and hoisted the body across the saddle; then he led the animal down the road to his horse. Mounting up, he returned to the Carlson ranch, where he put Frable's body on the horse tethered outside the barn. Leading the two horses, he rode back toward the camp.

Chapter Twelve

That night, Vince Bolton was unable to sleep. The bullet graze on his side had become sore, and a sharp pain stabbed him every time he moved. But that was not the only cause of his unease; he sensed that something was wrong, and he could not guess what it could be.

When the position of the stars indicated that dawn was near, he rose from his bedroll and built up the fire. The soldiers also were stirring, preparing to make coffee on another fire, and servants were beginning to move about as well. Still feeling uneasy, Vince went to check on the eight prisoners they had taken after the shoot-out with Congor's men. When he saw they were still sleeping, he walked to the eastern perimeter of the camp to wait for dawn. When it came, all movement in the camp ceased and all eyes turned to the eastern horizon.

The crest of a low hill three hundred yards away was covered with a line of Indians, about forty in all. The Indians were motionless and menacing, scorning any attempt at concealment. They were twice as numerous as the soldiers, and they were fully mobile, while the troop was burdened with having to defend the civilians and vehicles, which were in an exposed position.

As the sun rose, Vince peered through his binoculars at the Indians, trying to make out details against the bright glare. The others gathered behind him, speculat-

ing about the Indians and their intentions. Then Vince
identified the chief.

"It's White Eagle and his warriors," he said as he
turned to Henshaw. "I'll go parley with him and see if I
can reason with him. I'll need a volunteer to carry a
white flag on a staff. Get my horse saddled and the
volunteer ready, Sergeant. Then I'll talk with you about
battle plans."

Vince scanned the binoculars across the line of Indians again and then moved the glasses back to the one
standing beside the chief. Recognizing the tall half-
breed from the ambush at Manatial Lobo, Vince realized that, without a doubt, White Eagle intended to
retaliate for the virtual annihilation of the foraging
party.

Once his horse was saddled and a soldier was ready
with a white flag, Vince stepped aside with Henshaw
and told him he had spotted the half-breed. "As the
leading warrior in charge of that foraging party, the
half-breed ignored the chief's instructions. He must
have lied his way out of that, or he wouldn't be here at
all.

"I want you to get the three best riders ready to go for
help," Vince continued, "and each of them is to lead
two spare horses. One will go north around the mountains, one will go south, and the other will go across on
the road. Of the three, one should be able to outrun the
Indians."

"Yes, sir," Henshaw said. "When do you want them to
ride out?"

"If the Indians kill me and the trooper with the flag,
send the riders. If White Eagle won't make peace but
allows me to return, I'll have the man with the flag dip it
as a signal. That'll give the riders a head start of about
three hundred yards on the Indians."

"Good luck, sir," Henshaw said, and saluted.

Vince saluted the sergeant and then stepped to his
horse. The soldier with the white flag trembled visibly

as he waited beside his mount. "It won't do to let the Indians think you're afraid, Jessup," Vince warned him.

"I'll do my best to fool them, sir," the young man replied.

Vince laughed at the candid answer and mounted up. "I can't ask for any more than your best, son. Let's go."

The soldier stepped into his saddle and followed Vince. In order to reassure the people, Vince maintained an air of confidence that he did not feel. They looked up at him as he passed, some silently nodding and others wishing him good luck. Touching his hat, he smiled at Arabella, and she smiled wanly in reply.

Leaving the camp behind, he cantered toward the Indians, the white flag fluttering on the staff that the young trooper carried. Keen awareness of the peril hanging over Arabella and the others tugged at Vince's mind, and he tried to concentrate on the knowledge that White Eagle was a fair, reasonable man. It was difficult, because the hostility of the Indians was so intense that it was almost a tangible force as Vince approached them. The half-breed started to lift his rifle but then lowered it again as White Eagle glanced at him.

Vince reined up, saluting and greeting the chief in Spanish. "I am honored to meet with you again, White Eagle."

The old man nodded, but his bronzed, wrinkled face remained stony. His eyes were angry, yet they also reflected the mutual respect he and Vince had always shared. Gesturing toward Vince's shoulder, he acknowledged that Vince had been promoted from lieutenant to captain since their last meeting. "You have grown among your people, Vincent Bolton."

"You are the same, White Eagle, a Mescalero chief."

The remark was an expression of esteem, and the chief accepted it with another nod.

Then the half-breed spoke. "The horse soldier has grown among his people by killing our Indian brothers," he muttered.

"Perhaps," White Eagle agreed impassively, "and perhaps also through showing respect for his superiors by knowing when to remain silent."

The half-breed frowned darkly and looked away. Vince noticed that the reprimand created amusement among some of the warriors, revealing that the half-breed was not universally liked and respected by them. It was a promising sign, indicating at least a possibility that whatever the half-breed had said could be refuted.

The momentary satisfaction that Vince felt immediately evaporated, as the chief bluntly accused him and those with him of violating the sacred ground at Chupadera Mesa. Replying at length, Vince told the chief of Don Raimundo and Arabella and his reason for taking the Spaniards to the mesa.

"You still desecrated the sacred ground," the chief insisted.

"Is going there for this reason an act of desecration? I think not, White Eagle. The Spaniards wanted to take the remains of their ancient relative to their own sacred ground. That is a reason the spirits of the mesa can understand, and I believe you understand it, also."

Making no reply to the point, the chief asked, "Were the remains of the Spaniards' relative all that you carried away from the mesa?"

Vince shook his head, explaining that the priest had been accompanied by two companions, whose remains had also been removed. "The three Spaniards took food containers and gold from Gran Quivira. We carried away all that was in the cave with the remains of the Spaniards' relative and the other men."

"Did you or any of those with you go near the ancient houses where the spirits of the mesa live?"

"One did, but he is no longer with us. He took the gold and left, and I have sworn to kill him."

As the chief pondered this, the half-breed turned to him. "Lies, all lies!" he hissed angrily. "The horse soldier and the others went to Chupadera Mesa and desecrated the sacred ground to get gold! They and others fight over it like dogs!" He stabbed a finger toward the arroyo where Congor's men had been. "Yesterday, a battle was fought there for gold! It was all for gold, only gold!"

"We were attacked yesterday," Vince told the chief, "by those who thought we had gold. As I told you, it was taken, and we care nothing about it. We wish only to go in peace with the remains of the Spaniards."

White Eagle, his eyes cold, turned to the half-breed and said firmly, "Vincent Bolton tells the truth about this. He has told the truth about things he has no way of knowing that we know, so I believe him." He turned back to Vince. "The man Murillo is dead. We found him and learned that he had been at Chupadera Mesa. We took him to the mesa and buried him there with the gold."

Vince was momentarily dumbfounded. Regaining his composure, he said, "Then you did me a service. Do you agree that I took the Spaniards to Chupadera Mesa for a good reason?"

"The spirits of the mesa have been appeased," the chief replied, dismissing the subject with a gesture. "And the man Murillo was buried at the mesa to mollify the spirits, not as a service to you." He pointed to the half-breed. "This is Dark Cloud, a leading warrior. He told me that he and his foraging party approached you in peace, asking for food, and you killed his warriors. What do you say?"

"I say that Dark Cloud is a liar."

Snarling wordlessly in rage, the half-breed lifted his rifle. White Eagle reached out and pushed the barrel of the rifle down and glared at the leading warrior. Then he turned back to Vince. "I will listen to proof that Dark Cloud lied about what happened."

The half-breed glowered, sneering and occasionally grunting with disdain as Vince talked for several minutes. He described what he had found at the Carlson ranch and then told the chief about the theft of the horses and the ambush he had set up at the spring.

When he finished, the chief shrugged. "I have heard Dark Cloud speak, and I have heard you speak, Vincent Bolton. But I have heard no proof that Dark Cloud lied."

"I can take you to the ranch," Vince offered, "which is a short distance from here. A man, woman, youth, and two children were killed there. You will see a burned house and Mescalero arrows."

"If a ranch was attacked, he did it!" Dark Cloud barked, pointing to Vince. "When my warriors were killed, they had quivers full of arrows. He took them and attacked the ranch to place the blame on my foraging party! He merely wishes to escape retaliation for what he did!"

Vince laughed dryly, shaking his head. "White Eagle, do you believe I would do what Dark Cloud said?"

"I think not," the chief replied. "I also think that a leading warrior would not disobey my orders and attack a ranch. In one way or the other, I must be wrong. It is up to you to show me the way in which I am wrong, Vincent Bolton. I am waiting for proof that Dark Cloud lied."

As Dark Cloud smiled sardonically, Vince searched for some fact that the leading warrior would be unable to explain away. Then he thought of the second Indian who had survived the ambush at the spring, riding away with the half-breed. Any inconsistencies between what he and Dark Cloud said would at least make White Eagle suspicious.

"Where is the other warrior who rode away from Manatial Lobo with Dark Cloud?" Vince asked, looking around at the Indians. "If he is here, let me see his face and hear what he has to say."

For the first time, the chief's wrinkled face showed a surprised reaction. A murmur passed through the line of warriors as they frowned and exchanged glances. The half-breed's face, turning pale with consternation, was more revealing than that of the other Indians, and Vince knew he had found the key issue he needed.

When the leading warrior began angrily ranting in Apache, the chief silenced him with a gesture. "Dark Cloud told me that you and your soldiers killed all of his warriors."

"Dark Cloud lied," Vince replied, and then he added the obvious conclusion. "There was a witness who could tell you what Dark Cloud had actually done, so Dark Cloud killed him."

The half-breed growled in fury, again lifting his rifle. His finger was closing on the trigger when White Eagle leaned over from where he sat his horse, grasped the rifle, and lifted the barrel; then it fired, the bullet flying harmlessly through the air. The chief wrested the rifle away from Dark Cloud and glared at him. Throwing the rifle to the ground, White Eagle turned back to Vince. "I still wait for proof that Dark Cloud lied, Vincent Bolton," he said.

"The dead will speak and prove him a liar," Vince replied. He pointed toward the stagecoach and wagons. "I will tell these people to remain here while I ride with you and your warriors to Manatial Lobo. Somewhere south of the spring we will find what wild animals have left of a warrior's body."

"He put the body there, White Eagle!" Dark Cloud shouted, his face pale and beaded with perspiration as he pointed to Vince.

"Why do you have the sweat of guilt on your face?" White Eagle retorted. "You returned to the encampment with Running Deer's horse and your own. If we find his bones, they will speak, because I will know them. Now be silent."

The half-breed quieted, his anxiety evident as the chief thought for a moment. Then he spoke quietly to Vince. "I will give you a choice, Vincent Bolton," he said. "You may ride back to your people, and you will die honorably in battle. Or you may ride with us to Manatial Lobo to search for Running Deer's bones. If we do not find them, you will die there, and it will be a dishonorable and very painful death."

"I will go with you to Manatial Lobo," Vince replied.

The chief turned to the half-breed, speaking in the same quiet voice. "I will give you a choice, Dark Cloud. You may try to run from death here and now. Or you may ride with us to Manatial Lobo to search for Running Deer's bones. If we find them, your suffering will be so great that you will beg to die for many days before death brings you relief."

His face blanching, the half-breed looked around like a trapped animal. Suddenly he leaned low over his horse, drumming its ribs with his heels. As the horse raced away, White Eagle looked at the warriors and pointed. Rifles fired in a volley as arrows darted through the air. Then Dark Cloud tumbled from the horse, riddled with bullets and arrows.

One of the warriors went to catch the horse, while another one picked up the rifle from the ground. White Eagle gathered up his reins, lifting his right hand. "We part in peace, Vincent Bolton," he said, "but do not go to Chupadera Mesa again."

"I will not. Stay for a moment, White Eagle, and let us talk further. I will talk to the leader of the soldiers in Santa Fe and explain what happened, but soldiers may still come here because Dark Cloud's foraging party killed the people at the ranch. Eventually, they are certain to come. Your foraging parties take livestock from farms and ranches, which will bring soldiers here. Return to the reservation, White Eagle."

"No, I will not," the chief replied firmly. "I wish to live as my ancestors did, Vincent Bolton."

"I understand that, but others wish to live unmolested as farmers and ranchers. Both cannot be done, and the days of your ancestors are gone. Time passes and things change, White Eagle. It is time for you to return to the reservation."

"No. If the soldiers come, I will fight, like Geronimo."

"Geronimo will either return to the reservation or be killed. We both know that, because it's as plain as the sun that stands in the sky." Vince pointed to the warriors. "Will you make widows of their wives and orphans of their children? Your warriors are brave, but they will die. Return to the reservation, White Eagle."

The aged man was silent for a long moment, looking sadly into the distance. Then he sighed and shrugged. "I will think about what you have said, Vincent Bolton, and perhaps we will meet and talk again." He raised his right hand. "We part in peace."

Lifting his right hand, Vince replied, "We part in peace."

That evening camp was made in the lower foothills where the road began. Balmy temperatures replaced the torrid heat of the flatlands, invigorating the caravan. The vehicles traveled up the road at a fast walk the next day, and the column reached a wide creek during the afternoon. As he had planned, Vince made camp there for a few days so the wounded soldiers could recover somewhat before the journey across the mountains resumed. He was eager for some rest, as well, since the wound in his side was constantly bothering him.

Camp was made in a comfortable, wooded setting, with fresh, cold water once more in abundance. Vines hung heavy with ripe berries, and fish from the creek and game promised a welcome change of diet.

Sentries were posted, and two soldiers were designated to guard the eight outlaws. Then, after lines were filled with freshly laundered clothes hanging up to dry and other chores were done, the people happily settled down to an enjoyable respite from the journey.

Some of the drivers and soldiers went hunting or fishing, while others rested in the shade. Vince and Arabella picked berries for the cook to use for dessert, finding plump, juicy ones on the edge of a meadow near the camp. With only the last part of the journey remaining, each moment Vince spent with Arabella was precious to him, and sunset came much too quickly.

After breakfast the next morning, Vince and Arabella walked up the creek to pan for gold. Wearing a summery yellow dress, with the sunshine through the trees along the creek dappling her lovely face and thick, glossy hair, she had never been more captivating. She was as charming and vivacious as always, and he keenly enjoyed listening to her sweet, musical voice as she chatted with him in her liquid Castilian accent.

Vince taught her to pan for gold, enjoying her shoulder touching his arm and her soft, slender hands on the edge of the pan near his. When she washed a pan of gravel on her own and found a tiny nugget, her excitement and delight made him feel as happy as the gold made her feel.

As they walked on up the creek to look for other promising riffles, she took charge of the pan and carried it. Thinking about how much she enjoyed it, Vince warned her not ever to wander off by herself to pan for gold. She laughed lightly, shaking her head. "No, I won't," she assured him. "I incurred your brutal temper once, and I won't do that again."

"Brutal temper?" he exclaimed. "Arabella, I admit that I acted too harshly when I became angry at you, and I apologize for it. But really, I have a very even temper."

"Vincent, Vincent," she chided him, amused. "Please don't deny what I have seen with my own eyes. That was not the only time I have seen you angry. On the night that Murillo fled with the gold, you were like a wild beast of the forest, all because he had outwitted you."

"Outwitted me? Well, it was foolish of me not to have searched him more thoroughly for weapons, but that wasn't why I was angry. I was angry because of what he did to you."

Arabella stopped and turned, looking up at him. "Because of what he did to me, Vincent?"

"Yes, he threatened your life, and he . . . well, he put his hands on you. That's why I was angry. I thought you knew that."

She smiled, shaking her head. "No, I did not. How was I to know, Vincent? You did not tell me."

"No, but I thought you knew."

Arabella shook her head again, smiling up at him and hesitating for a moment. Then she turned and walked on. "I am very flattered and pleased, Vincent," she said, glancing around. "Is it not lovely here? One can well understand why people love this country."

"I do, and people who come from far and wide do as well. And as you know, many people from Spain made their homes here."

"Yes, and I am sure they loved Spain as much as I do," she commented. "But I can understand why they would be happy here."

As they walked on up the creek, Vince thought about the times she had talked about things she would like to do in New Mexico Territory. He wondered if such a sophisticated, cosmopolitan young woman could ever be content to give up all she had known to live in the West.

The train of thought led him to speculate whether the undeniable attraction he felt for her was as powerful a force in her, and whether she would ever consider marrying him. The idea of asking her created a shrinking fear within him that he had never experienced before, not even while leading a cavalry charge into volleys of gunfire. Suddenly he felt that he had to know one way or the other. Twice he opened his mouth to ask her, but both times he was unable to utter the words. Then the words came out unbidden, almost against his will.

"Arabella, will you marry me?" he blurted.

Dropping the pan with a clatter, she put her hands to her face and stopped so suddenly that Vince almost ran into her. With her back to him she stood unmoving for a moment, and he was perplexed by her reaction. "Have I shocked you?" he asked uneasily. "Perhaps I spoke too suddenly. . . ."

"I am not shocked; I am relieved!" she exclaimed,

turning. "Vincent, I was beginning to think that *I* would have to ask *you*!"

"Ask me?" he echoed blankly.

"Yes!" she replied with exasperation. "I have devised countless ways to tell you I wanted to stay here, and I was shamelessly bold. Even then, though, you said nothing. I could see what you were thinking, but you never spoke one word about it to me."

"I was afraid you would refuse," he confessed.

"How could I?" she said, smiling radiantly. "I love you, and I want nothing more than to be your wife, Vincent."

Then she was in his arms, warm and fragrant, and his lips were on hers. After the weeks of having loved her deeply with the near certainty that she could never be his, it was difficult for him to believe that she had actually said she wanted to marry him. He held her close and kissed her ardently in the most blissfully joyful moment of his life. He felt as if he had reached for the stars and somehow grasped the most precious one of all.

They moved to a log beside the creek and sat down together. Arabella snuggled close in his arms, and Vince caressed her long, blue-black hair. Happiness seemed so simple as they talked. The quarters at his fort in Arizona Territory were spartan, and other things would be different from what she had known, but she told him she could be perfectly happy there as his wife.

Then a dark shadow of uncertainty materialized again when he mentioned asking her father's permission. Arabella's smile faded as she shook her head. "No, no, that will not do at all, Vincent," she said firmly. "We must prepare very carefully to ask his permission."

"Might he refuse us permission to marry?"

"Indeed he may," Arabella replied somberly. "He talks about how much latitude I have in what I do, and I do have great freedom compared to others. But on important issues, he makes the decisions. It took weeks of persuasion for him to allow me to accompany him here."

"And we don't have many weeks," Vince mused, pondering the obstacle that still stood between them. "On a couple of occasions he's mentioned the Duke of Valencia's proposal of marriage. He seems to regard it very favorably."

"He does. It would be an advantageous marriage for both families, but my father's main concern is my happiness. His feelings for you are similar to those he has for his sons, which is a far greater fondness than he feels for the duke. But he will question whether I could be happy with you over the years to come."

Vince sighed, nodding. "Well, do you think we should wait until we reach Socorro to ask him?"

"Yes, and then wait until he has rested. The journey is very tiring for him, and he will be more open to persuasion when he is comfortable. In the meantime, I will try to drop small hints and prepare him."

Vince could not bring himself to ask Arabella what she would do if her father refused permission—it was impossible to think of a life without her. He kissed her again, trying to be optimistic. But with the one thing in his life that meant the most to him at stake, he was unable to dismiss his anxiety.

Chapter Thirteen

In the choir loft of San Miguel Church in Socorro, the organ pealed out the first notes of the *Agnus Dei*, and the boys' choir joined in with their clear soprano voices. At the front of the center aisle, the rosewood box lay on a table covered by black velvet that was emblazoned with the Carranza crest in gold. It was flanked by the remains of the friars, now in polished oak boxes. Incense vapor wafted around the altar, where the bishop and the assisting priests moved about in their rich vestments. The quiet of the large congregation reflected the solemnity of the occasion, which had drawn all the dignitaries in the territory, as well as officials from Washington. Vince and his father sat on the second bench, with the governor, his staff, and their wives.

In contrast to the others, the front bench was empty except for Don Raimundo and Arabella. Wearing a dress of black satin with an arabesque design and a black mantilla, she clasped her rosary in her hands and closed her eyes. As the majestic music swelled, Don Raimundo put his handkerchief to his face to blot his tears.

Well aware of the importance of the service to the aged grandee, Vince knew he was overcome with joy. In an ornate, magnificent church that had been a simple adobe chapel when they had undoubtedly visited it two centuries before, Padre Eusebio and his faithful companions were being returned to the embrace of the cause for which they had died as martyrs. The last hymn was sung, and the ceremony drew to an end with the bishop's giving the final blessing.

As the organ played softly and the congregation filed out, the bishop and priests came down from the altar to talk with Don Raimundo and Arabella. Vince stepped around to the front bench and stood by her side. He had yet to ask her father's permission to marry her, and even as he admired her beauty, he thought of the problems the grandee would consider. Her rosary was made of the finest ebony beads alternating with gems, and the heavy gold cross that hung from it was set with large diamonds. Her mantilla was made from yards of lavish, expensive lace and reached the hem of her dress. Either of the items had cost in the range of a year's pay for Vince, something that Don Raimundo was certain to take into account.

The bishop and priests promised to be at the opening of the public celebration at sunset that day, and then they also withdrew. As Vince started to leave with his father and the Carranzas, the governor touched his arm and beckoned him aside. As Harvey and the Carranzas went ahead, Vince spoke briefly with the governor and Colonel Hamilton.

"The colonel and I have read your report with great interest," Governor Sheldon explained. "We would like to talk with you at your very earliest convenience about a subject that is touched upon in your report."

"Very well, sir. I'll be at your hotel in half an hour."

Vince caught up with the others at the door and told them of the governor's request. He helped Arabella and her father into a coach from the way station and then said, "I don't know how long the discussion will last, but I'm sure it'll be over before the public celebration begins. Governor Sheldon and Colonel Hamilton won't want to miss that."

The remarks were mainly for Arabella's benefit, as she and Vince had been looking forward to the afternoon. Her smile was regretful as she waved good-bye, but she accepted what had to be done; like her father, she understood that duty must come before pleasure. It was one of the many things about her that Vince appreciated.

Vince turned to his father, who was driving the coach, and said, "I'm sure I won't be gone long, Dad."

Harvey Bolton replied, "I should hope not, son. Don't let them keep you from the festivities for too long. That fancy uniform should be good for something." He nodded toward the gold-leaf insignia on Vince's shoulders. The day after arriving back in Socorro, Vince had received a telegram from the army chief of staff congratulating him on his success and informing him of his promotion to major.

Vince rode across the compound and out the gate. Since his return to Socorro, he had found that he was something of a celebrity. As he rode along the streets, people shouted and waved for a reason he also found deeply gratifying. He had rid the town of Big Jim Congor.

After tethering his horse to the hitch rail in front of the hotel, Vince went inside and upstairs to the governor's suite. Relaxing in his shirtsleeves, Governor Sheldon opened the door when Vince knocked. "Come in, Major Bolton," he said amiably. "Thank you for being so prompt. Make yourself comfortable."

Stepping into the sitting room of the suite, Vince exchanged a nod of greeting with Colonel Hamilton, who was seated on the couch. The governor took Vince's hat and showed him to a chair. Then he went to a sideboard, where he took out the thick report on the journey that Vince had sent to Santa Fe. Sheldon sat down in a chair, thumbing through the report.

Finding the section in which Vince described his meeting with White Eagle, Sheldon said, "This is the first time I've seen any promise for a satisfactory solution to the problem." Then referring to the chief's attempts to keep his foraging parties from attacking settlers, the governor said that he, in turn, had been

very circumspect toward the Mescaleros. Farmers and
ranchers had complained bitterly about having their
livestock stolen, but the governor had resisted mounting a campaign against White Eagle.

"We're afraid that if we begin military action, we'll
end up having another Geronimo on our hands," he
summed up frankly. "We could have the same situation
here that exists in Arizona Territory."

"Washington knows that, too," Hamilton added.
"This is a matter of concern at the highest levels."

The governor continued. "At the end of your conversation with White Eagle, the chief didn't rule out returning to the reservation, correct?"

"He didn't rule it out absolutely," Vince answered,
"but he definitely wasn't in favor of it, sir."

"But his reaction appears very promising," the governor insisted. "What I consider even more favorable is
your presence in the area. You know the Indians here,
and even better, you and White Eagle are friends."

"Not quite, sir," Vince replied firmly. "He and I respect each other, but that's all. We're not friends."

"But your dealings with the chief have never esca-
lated to violence, Major, and you last parted with him
on peaceful terms. As far as I'm concerned, that's
friendly enough."

The governor continued, taking the broadest and
most optimistic view of what Vince had written. Then
he clearly stated what Vince had been expecting to
hear: He wanted Vince to meet with White Eagle and
talk him into returning to the reservation with his warriors.

Vince's uncertainty about Don Raimundo's permission to marry Arabella was uppermost in his thoughts,
and he was reluctant even to consider other commit-
ments before he knew what the grandee's answer
would be. At the same time, his sense of duty reminded
him that the governor was right; White Eagle could end
up causing the same problems here that Geronimo was
creating in Arizona Territory.

The governor talked on, saying that he would provide funds to buy gifts for the Indians and any other assistance Vince needed. Hamilton added that Vince would have a cavalry escort at his disposal.

"Well, I'd like to think about it, if I may," Vince said.

"Of course," Hamilton replied briskly. "Even though you've just been promoted, persuading White Eagle to return to the reservation could very well put you in line for another one," he pointed out. "But time isn't particularly critical, so take a few days to think it over." He took out his watch and looked at it. "Speaking of time, if we don't hurry, we'll be late for the celebration that Don Raimundo is hosting."

Vince stood up, made his parting remarks to the two men, and then left. As he rode back toward the way station in the late afternoon sunlight, he thought about what the governor wanted him to do. He considered his chances of success at least fair, and it would be a service of great value to the territory if he did succeed. However, in respect to his personal affairs, the request had come at a very inopportune time.

At the way station, townspeople were gathering outside the gate in a hubbub of excited conversation and laughter, waiting for the celebration to begin. Beef and pork turned slowly on spits over fires, and cooks were bustling about, stirring large pans of simmering vegetables. Casks of beverages were sitting on trestle tables, along with fruit and desserts. The mariachi band had arrived, and the musicians were setting up on the bandstand. Don Raimundo had spared no expense in providing Socorro with a fiesta that would be remembered for years.

Luminaries lined the eaves of the buildings and the top of the wall around the compound, brightening as the sun set. As the governor and other dignitaries arrived, a crowd of people flooded in the gate. Joining his father, Vince went there to meet them and then walked

oward the bandstand to wait for Don Raimundo to
nake his appearance.

As they reached the bandstand, Don Raimundo and
Arabella entered the compound. She was bewitching in
a blue gown and shawl, but at a glance, Vince knew
something was wrong. Her smile was wan, her eyes
troubled.

The grandee's wrinkled face revealed nothing as
Vince helped him up the steps to the bandstand. The
crowd fell silent as he spoke briefly in Castilian Spanish,
thanking them for coming and expressing his hope that
they would enjoy the celebration. The governor joined
him on the dais to thank him on behalf of everyone for
hosting the fiesta, and then Sheldon assisted Don Raimundo back down the steps.

The band struck up a lively tune and people began to
dance. Vince and Arabella followed her father and the
governor toward their table, where wineglasses were
being filled. When they were seated, Arabella at last
had a chance to whisper a few words to Vince. A short
time before, she explained, she had dropped a hint to
her father about how fond she was of Vince, as she had
been doing during the past days.

"I must have said too much," she continued anxiously. "He asked me exactly what I meant, and I was
terrified, at a loss for words. Then he told me he wanted
to speak with the two of us soon."

Deeply distressed, Vince tried to conceal his feelings
so as not to worry Arabella. He squeezed her hand under the table and whispered to her, "We will find a way
to be together, my darling."

The governor gave a toast and then talked with Don
Raimundo in his limited Spanish as the two of them
sipped their wine. Vince filled glasses for himself and
Arabella, but they remained untouched as the couple
waited. Presently Don Raimundo put his glass aside and
withdrew, glancing meaningfully at Arabella. She and
Vince followed him as he went toward his room.

The muffled sound of the music and gaiety outside

came through the door as Don Raimundo turned up the lamp on a table and sat down on a couch, pointing to chairs. "Please, sit down. Major, I believe the relationship between you and my daughter has proceeded beyond friendship. If so, would you like to discuss it with me?"

"I'm grateful for the opportunity to do so," Vince replied as he and Arabella sat down. Then he plunged on. "Arabella and I love each other, and I would like to have your permission for us to marry."

The grandee sighed and then smiled regretfully. "I am more fond of you than of any man other than my sons, Major," he said. "I believe you are fond of me, also, and I truly hope that it will not destroy our friendship, but I hesitate to grant permission."

Vince's heart was racing, and his throat was dry. Swallowing hard, he said, "May I ask why, Don Raimundo?"

"As a cavalry officer stationed in forts in this region, you need a wife who can endure privation as a way of life. Arabella is not pampered, but she is accustomed to wealth. She needs a husband who can provide that."

"Father, I do not," Arabella said bluntly. "Vincent and I love each other, and that is all that I need and want in a marriage."

"Yes, for the present," the grandee replied. "Perhaps even for a year or two. But marriage is for life, my dear. Love is a fragile flower that will wither and die under harsh conditions, when you are deprived of what you have always had."

"Don Raimundo," Vince implored, "the love that Arabella and I have for each other is far more sturdy than a fragile flower. I promise you that it will easily endure whatever tests and trials it must. And while I can't give Arabella all she has known, as the wife of an army major she will not live in poverty."

The grandee hesitated for a moment and then said, "But you do not have the means to make life at an army fort comparable to what Arabella has always known.

er love may be strong, but not strong enough to en-
ure that."

"It is, Father," Arabella said quietly, but her tone was
rm. "You know how much I love you, and my love for
incent is so strong that I will willingly stay behind
hen you leave. I will give up my country and make
is one mine. My love is so strong that I will give up
hatever I must to be Vincent's wife."

"But you do not know what you will give up!" her
ther objected. "You have never experienced want, so
is outside your comprehension."

"With all respect, Don Raimundo," Vince put in, "I
elieve you underestimate Arabella. Many people from
pain made their homes here under conditions more
evere than now, some from families like yours."

The aged man pondered again for a moment and
en smiled wryly. "You are very persuasive, Vincent,"
e admitted. "But if I give permission for my daughter
o marry, it will be a decision that commits her to a
ituation in which I am not sure she will be happy."

"I agree that this is a decision of great importance to
er," Vince pointed out. "But if you refuse us permis-
ion to marry, you will be committing Arabella to un-
appiness. I believe you can see that now."

"Yes, I can," the grandee agreed, turning to Arabella.
Ie paused and then slowly nodded. "Very well, you
nay marry. I will remain here for the wedding—and to
rrange a dowry of half a million American dollars."

A radiant smile of delight wreathed Arabella's face,
nd she gasped in joy.

His expression transforming into a broad smile, Don
Raimundo embraced his daughter and future son-in-
aw. "I should think that will make the transition a little
asier on you, Arabella."

Vince's pleasure matched Arabella's at first, but he
ecame more restrained when he thought about the
enerous dowry. As a matter of pride, he wanted to
upport his family himself.

"You'll never regret your decision," Vince assured

the grandee. "If you would like to give Arabella a st
pend for herself, I certainly have no objection, but pr
viding a dowry isn't necessary."

"It is necessary if you wish to marry Arabella, Vin
cent," Don Raimundo replied firmly. "It is a conditio
to my giving permission for her to marry you. Regar
less of her assurances about being able to give up wha
she has always had, I intend to be certain that she wi
be happy."

Given a choice between his pride and Arabella, Vinc
had no hesitation. "Very well, Don Raimundo, as yo
wish."

"I appreciate your acceding to my wishes, Vincent
And now, my children, we must go to join the others i
celebration. We have so much more to celebrate now
You two go on. I will join you in a few moments."

Taking their leave of the grandee, Vince and Arabell
walked arm in arm from his room. Leading her to th
shadows at the end of the building, Vince took her in hi
arms and kissed her. They gazed at each other for
moment in silence, their eyes expressing all the joy the
felt. Then they walked back toward the crowd.

"Would you care for something to eat or drink?
Vince asked.

"No, I am much too excited to eat or drink. Let
dance, Vincent."

Joining the other couples in front of the bandstand
they began dancing as they talked. Arabella asked wha
the governor had wanted, wondering if it would inter
fere with their marriage plans. Vince told her of th
governor's plans and explained that he would be able t
defer it until after they were married. "After the wed
ding," he continued, "we can rent a house here i
Socorro for a time."

They discussed the date of the ceremony, and then
Arabella pursued the subject of the conference with
White Eagle. "How will you arrange the meeting?" she
asked.

"Well, I know all of the chiefs at the Mescalero reser-

ation, so I'll ask one of them to send word to White
Eagle that I want to talk with him. Then we'll meet
somewhere in the flatlands, probably at the spring I told
you about, Manatial Lobo. I don't know how long all
that will take, but I'll be back as soon as possible."

"You can take as long as you wish, Vincent, because
you will not be gone from me at all. I will go with you."

He started to laugh until he saw she was serious. Then
he stopped dancing so suddenly that other dancers
brushed against them. Leading Arabella to one side of
the dancers, he told her firmly that she would have to
stay in Socorro. "It won't be any sort of vacation, Arabella," he said sternly. "In addition, it could be dangerous, and I'm not about to take you into a situation like
that."

"Are you going to vent your savage temper on me
now, Vincent?" she asked, looking up at him placidly.
"Do you intend to berate me here in the presence of all
these people? If you do that before we are married,
what sort of indignities must I suffer after we are married?"

People nearby were turning to look at the couple.
Vince led Arabella back among the dancers and began
dancing with her again, both annoyed and amused as he
reconsidered. Then he shrugged and acquiesced.

"Thank you, Vincent," she replied, smiling happily.
"I promise that I will not be any trouble."

Vince laughed, giving up and nodding. Remember-
ing that Don Raimundo had said the Duke of Valencia's
life would not be dull if he married Arabella, Vince
reflected that now his own life with her was going to be
anything but boring. But he knew that every moment
of it would be fascinating.

★ WAGONS WEST ★

This continuing, magnificent saga recounts the adventures of a brave
band of settlers, all of different backgrounds, all sharing one dream—
to find a new and better life.

☐	26822	INDEPENDENCE! #1	$4.50
☐	26162	NEBRASKA! #2	$4.50
☐	26242	WYOMING! #3	$4.50
☐	26072	OREGON! #4	$4.50
☐	26070	TEXAS! #5	$4.50
☐	26377	CALIFORNIA! #6	$4.50
☐	26546	COLORADO! #7	$4.50
☐	26069	NEVADA! #8	$4.50
☐	26163	WASHINGTON! #9	$4.50
☐	26073	MONTANA! #10	$4.50
☐	26184	DAKOTA! #11	$4.50
☐	26521	UTAH! #12	$4.50
☐	26071	IDAHO! #13	$4.50
☐	26367	MISSOURI! #14	$4.50
☐	27141	MISSISSIPPI! #15	$4.50
☐	25247	LOUISIANA! #16	$4.50
☐	25622	TENNESSEE! #17	$4.50
☐	26022	ILLINOIS! #18	$4.50
☐	26533	WISCONSIN! #19	$4.50
☐	26849	KENTUCKY! #20	$4.50
☐	27065	ARIZONA! #21	$4.50
☐	27458	NEW MEXICO! #22	$4.50
☐	27703	OKLAHOMA! #23	$4.50

THE EXCITING NEW FRONTIER SERIES
BY THE CREATORS OF
WAGONS WEST

STAGECOACH
by Hank Mitchum

"The STAGECOACH series is great frontier entertainment. Hank Mitchum really makes the West come alive in each story."
        —*Dana Fuller Ross, author of Wagons West*

**FROM THE PRODUCER OF WAGONS WEST
AND THE KENT FAMILY CHRONICLES—
A SWEEPING SAGA OF WAR AND HEROISM
AT THE BIRTH OF A NATION**

THE WHITE INDIAN SERIES

This thrilling series tells the compelling story of America's birth against the equally exciting adventures of an English child raised as a Seneca.

☐	24650	White Indian #1	$3.95
☐	25020	The Renegade #2	$3.95
☐	24751	War Chief #3	$3.95
☐	24476	The Sachem #4	$3.95
☐	25154	Renno #5	$3.95
☐	25039	Tomahawk #6	$3.95
☐	25589	War Cry #7	$3.95
☐	25202	Ambush #8	$3.95
☐	23986	Seneca #9	$3.95
☐	24492	Cherokee #10	$3.95
☐	24950	Choctaw #11	$3.95
☐	25353	Seminole #12	$3.95
☐	25868	War Drums #13	$3.95
☐	26206	Apache #14	$3.95
☐	27161	Spirit Knife #15	$3.95
☐	27264	Manitou #16	$3.95
☐	27814	Seneca Warrior #17	$3.95

Special Offer
Buy a Bantam Book
for only 50¢.

Now you can have Bantam's catalog filled with hundreds of titles plus take advantage of our unique and exciting bonus book offer. A special offer which gives you the opportunity to purchase a Bantam book for only 50¢. Here's how!

By ordering any five books at the regular price per order, you can also choose any other single book listed (up to a $5.95 value) for just 50¢. Some restrictions do apply, but for further details why not send for Bantam's catalog of titles today!

Just send us your name and address and we will send you a catalog!